Tales from Ballyclara

a collection of short stories
from the Aoife O'Reilly series

by Erin Bowlen

For Daddy
Who taught me (almost) everything I know about storytelling.

A Note from the Author

Dear reader,

One of the toughest parts about being a writer is picking and choosing which scenes make it into the final draft of a book, and which end up on the cutting room floor. The following short stories are from scenes that were cut from the first book in the Aoife O'Reilly series, *All That Compels the Heart*. All of them take place before Aoife's arrival in Ballyclara, starting with *Christmas in Ballyclara*, which takes place roughly ten years before we meet Aoife, up to *The Mystery of the Auburn-Haired Woman*, which takes place only weeks before her arrival.

At its heart, this collection is a series of stories about community. I hope you enjoy reading them as much as I enjoyed writing them.

Slàinte!

Table of Contents

Christmas in Ballyclara

Seventeen-year-old Mara Flanagan stood at the kitchen window, looking out at the green fields of Ballyclara, Ireland.

"Do ye think we'll get snow for Christmas this year, Mam?"

Her mother, Sinead, looked up from chopping carrots for the stew she was making.

"It's cold enough for it, that's for sure, but we haven't had snow at Christmas since you were young. I wouldn't hold your breath over it."

Mara's shoulders slumped.

"Besides, you don't want a white Christmas, do you? It just means shoveling snow and ice, and if the electricity goes out, well, I don't even want to think how we'd manage Christmas dinner, then. Now, come over here and help me finish this stew or we'll have nothing for supper, and you know what your grandad is like when his supper's late."

Mara sighed and returned to chopping the rest of the vegetables. She didn't know what it was about a white Christmas – maybe it was all the songs or American films – but she'd always thought a white Christmas was magical. The last one they'd had was one of her favourite Christmas memories, and she wanted to recapture that feeling. It had been a tough year for the Flanagans. Work had been hard to come by and Mara just felt that they could all use a little magic in their lives right now. Her thoughts were interrupted by the arrival of her younger brother.

"Ah, good, Michael, you're back. Were ye able to get everything on the list for tomorrow?" his mother asked him.

"Just barely. *O'Sullivan's* was mighty packed." He placed two large, brown shopping bags on the kitchen table.

"Mmhmm, that smells good!" He took a step closer to the stove, trying to peer into the soup pot.

"Get away from there!" his mother chastised, lightly hitting him with a dishtowel. "Now, go outside and tell your father he needs to come in and get dressed for church. It's almost time we were on our way."

"Ah, Mam! Can't we have our supper now before church?"

"Church first, supper later. You know this! Now, go on and hurry up or we'll be late. The later we are going to church, the later we are coming home from it, and the later you'll be for supper. So, get a move on."

Michael sighed and turned on his heel, heading back out into the cold.

"Mmhmm, something smells good," Dermot repeated his son's earlier sentiment a few minutes later, sniffing the air.

"Flanagan men, always guided by your stomachs," Sinead teased.

"Well, it's no wonder when it's your cooking we're talking about." Dermot came up to her and gave her a quick kiss on the cheek.

Sinead blushed. "You're a big flirt, Dermot Flanagan, so ye are! Now, off with the pair of ye. You need to wash up and get dressed for church. Mara, you too. Go on! We need to be ready to be out the door in ten minutes!"

Mara joined her brother and her father in ascending the staircase to the second floor of her parents' small cottage. Hurriedly, she put on her Christmas dress, a navy-blue one with spaghetti straps and a matching shawl she'd saved all her spare money for. As she slipped on her kitten heels, she quickly examined herself in the mirror. Grabbing a silver sparkling hair clip from her dresser, she gathered her long black hair up and pinned it into place.

"You look lovely, dear. That dress really suits you," Sinead said, stopping in quickly on her way to change out of her apron and workaday clothes.

"Thanks, Mam."

Mara bounded down the stairs, her brother already sitting on the chesterfield.

"Typical. Mam hurries us all along and then makes us wait," he grumbled.

Mara rolled her eyes at him. Her younger brother was so impatient that it was annoying, sometimes.

"They'll be down soon. See?" She nodded her head towards her father, who was already coming down the stairs.

"Ready to go?"

"Just waiting on Mam," Mara replied.

"She should be down any moment, so let's put on

our coats and boots and be ready for when she comes down."

"Well, what are ye all waiting for?" their mother exclaimed as she descended the stairs a few minutes later. "Let's get moving!"

"We were waiting on you, Mam," Michael replied, exasperated.

"Yes, well, I'm here now, so let's get a move on. We still need to go and get your grandfather." She ushered them out towards the car.

"Brrr…" Mara shivered as she settled into the back of the car, the fabric of the seat cold against the skin of her bare legs. She was regretting now that she hadn't worn tights.

Her father turned on the car, a blast of cold air blowing throughout the interior. The old car reluctantly eased out of the drive and headed down the lane towards her grandfather's house. It wasn't a long journey; Liam Flanagan only lived two cottages down from Sinead and Dermot's place. As they pulled into the drive, Dermot turned off the car again.

"Da! Turn the car back on. It was only just warming up!" Michael complained.

"We'll freeze out here!" Mara agreed with her brother, shivering a bit.

"I won't be a moment," her father replied. "Besides, it's bad for the environment to leave it running. That's what you and your brother are always telling me, anyhow."

Mara mentally cursed herself for lecturing her parents about being more environmentally conscious. It was all well and good to think about the environment when it was sunny and warm out, and it didn't interfere with your own comfort, but it was another matter entirely when you were sitting in the back of a freezing car.

A few minutes later, Dermot returned with their grandfather, who shuffled along slowly.

"Hello, Grandda," Mara greeted him as he settled himself in the backseat with her and Michael.

"You're late," he replied, buckling himself in.

"And a good evening to you as well," Sinead welcomed him from the front seat, non-plussed by his grumpy demeanour.

"Well, let's go," Liam barked.

"Yes, Da. We're on our way now," Dermot replied, trying to keep his patience. Mara always found it interesting to observe her father when he was around her grandfather. Suddenly, he went from parent to child in under a minute, and she found it highly amusing to see him being the one who got chastised.

"I want to be home to have my supper at a decent hour," Liam grumbled.

Mara noticed her mother giving her father a pointed look, as if to emphasize her earlier point about Flanagan men thinking with their stomachs. When they arrived at the church a few minutes later, the place was nearly full.

"There's Brendan and Molly over there," Mara pointed out to Michael, seeing Molly waving to her from their usual pew.

"Hey, Moll!" she greeted her friend, joining her and the rest of her family.

"Hey!"

The two friends caught up as the Flanagans settled themselves into the pew with them. They were talking animatedly about the exams they'd just completed before the Christmas break when their conversation was interrupted by the arrival of the Byrne family.

"Hey Mara."

She turned around and looked up into the handsome eyes of Alistair Byrne, captain of her secondary school's rugby team, and the cutest boy in her sixth-year class. He also happened to be Mara's secret boyfriend.

"Hey…hi…Alistair," she stuttered nervously. She mentally cursed her awkwardness. Even though the two of them had been dating for three weeks now, she still felt like a bumbling eejit around him.

Alistair smirked at her as he and his family sat down in the pew across from them. Mara let her eyes linger a little longer until she noticed his mother, Riona, glaring at her from behind Alistair's back.

"When are you going to ask him out?" Molly asked, nudging her in the side, forcing her to turn away from Riona's glare.

"Yeah, right. Like I'd have the courage to do that!" she whispered in reply.

In truth, she hadn't been the one to ask him out. She'd been totally floored when *he'd* asked *her* out after school a few weeks before. She hadn't thought he'd even noticed her before, so it had come as a big shock.

"Oh, come on! You've had a crush on him forever! It's time you said something," Molly insisted.

Mara blushed at the reminder of her long-time crush on Alistair Byrne. She wanted to tell Molly all about how the two of them were actually together, but she knew that, try as she might, Molly couldn't keep a secret from her boyfriend, Brendan, who'd end up telling his best friend, Michael, and then it would inevitably get back to her parents. And, while the Byrnes and the Flanagans were perfectly cordial neighbours, they weren't close. Mara didn't know the details, but it all went back to when her parents had been her age. All she knew was that Sinead found Riona to be pretentious, and Riona didn't exactly do anything to dispel the idea. And so, the two families remained polite, but they didn't socialize together.

Mara and Molly settled down when they heard the music for the service starting. However, much as she tried, Mara just couldn't focus on Father Patrick's service. The temptation to casually glance in Alistair's direction every few seconds was just too great. From the smug smile on his face, she was fairly certain he was very much aware of what she was doing. When her mother gave her a small nudge, she reluctantly peeled her eyes away from Alistair to glance over at Molly, who was making eyes at Brendan McCaffrey.

"Oh, stop, you two!" she teasingly whispered in Molly's ear.

"Like you're not doing the same with Alistair over there, making eyes at Alistair over there," Molly retorted.

Mara rolled her eyes at her.

Their chit-chat drew the attention of her mother, who shot her a "be quiet!" look. Mara heeded her mother's unspoken warning as Father Patrick launched into his sermon. She tried to pay attention, but at the end of the day, she was still a seventeen-year-old. There were only so many times she could hear the story of the birth of Jesus and not get a little bored. After two thousand years, how many new angles could the priest find to make it interesting?

As it turned out, her grandfather was thinking the same thing. Liam Flanagan had never been shy about letting Father Patrick know when he felt he was going on a bit too long with his service, and tonight was no exception. About ten minutes into the sermon, Liam began tapping his cane on the leg of the pew in front of him. It wasn't a loud tapping, just loud enough for the kindly priest to know what it meant. Mara watched as Father Patrick paused in the middle of his sentence, looked down at his notes in front of him, and then made the split-second decision to wrap up his sermon early.

"And so, the miracle of Christ. A very happy Christmas to you all."

Mara could hear Molly trying to stifle a giggle beside her as the choir launched into "O Come All Ye Faithful." She felt a wave of empathy for the priest as they stood to sing. No one enjoyed being on Liam Flanagan's cranky side. After the service, the Flanagans began their way to exit.

"Excellent service, Father." Dermot shook the priest's hand as they reached the door.

"Yes, even if it did go on a bit," Liam interjected.

"Thank ye, Dermot," Father Patrick replied, politely ignoring Liam's comment. "Say, could I interest anyone in a mug of mulled wine?"

"We would love to, Father," Sinead replied, ignoring the exasperated looks from her son and father-in-law.

"Ah, Mam, but we've got the stew back at home."

"Yes, and it'll still be there a few minutes from now," his mother chastised him. "You're being rude!"

"I'm nearly done here, but you all can go on down and let yourselves in. The door's open. I'll join you in a moment," Father Patrick said, smiling at them.

"Thank you, Father. We'll see you soon." Sinead ushered her family out into the chilly winter air.

Once they were outside, Mara overheard her brother asking their father if Brendan could stay the night.

"As long as your parents have no objections."

"They're totally fine with it, Mr. Flanagan," Brendan reassured him.

"If Michael gets to have Brendan stay over, then I want Molly to stay over too," Mara interrupted, linking arms with her best friend.

"And have you asked Molly if she wants to even stay over on Christmas Eve?" Sinead asked her. "What if she wants to spend Christmas Eve with her parents?"

"I'd love to stay over tonight, Mrs. Flanagan, if you don't mind, that is."

Mara caught her making eyes at Brendan and suspected that her enthusiasm was more than just the excitement of hanging out with her best friend.

"Of course, we don't mind, dear. Just make sure to ask your parents."

"Oh, they already said it was ok," Molly replied quickly. "I asked them earlier. I had a feeling that Mara was going to ask."

"Well, then. Since Father Patrick has invited us over to his place for a quick, festive drink, let's head down there first and then we can get you all home for supper."

The party moved towards the little cottage a hundred metres or so from the church. After he'd moved to Ballyclara, Father Patrick had decided that Aldridge Manor – also known as the Old Rectory to the locals – was too big a place for a single man such as himself, and the little, abandoned groundskeeper cottage would be much better suited to his needs. They entered the small cottage, warming themselves at the stone fireplace, the heady scent of the mulled wine filled wafting from the kitchen.

"Father Patrick has done it again. That mulled wine smells spectacular."

"Please, help yourselves." The temperature dropped a degree or two as Father Patrick opened the door to let himself in. "There's mugs in the cupboard right above your head."

Sinead obliged, bringing the mugs down and filling them with the warm drink.

"Oh, and there's sparkling apple juice in the refrigerator, too."

"Sparkling juice?" Michael asked, his tone incredulous.

"You're too young for alcohol," Sinead warned him.

"Ah, Mam! C'mon, it's Christmas," Mara and Michael both protested as she poured out the sparkling juice for the four teens.

"Ye can have some mulled wine in a couple of years when it's legal," his mother chastised. "Now, shall we toast to good friends and family, and a very Happy Christmas to all?"

"Slàinte!" the others chorused, sipping from their glasses.

Several minutes later, their drinks consumed, Liam and Michael were once again anxious again to get home to their dinner.

"Yes, yes. Alright, we're heading out," Sinead replied, after noticing the look her son was giving her. She gave Father Patrick an apologetic look.

"Supper?" Liam asked, loudly.

"Yes, Da. We're going to go home and have supper now," Dermot confirmed, looking slightly amused.

Liam enthusiastically rose to his feet, eager to get out of there.

"Thank ye for the hospitality, Father. Will we be seeing you tomorrow for Christmas dinner after church?"

"Only something truly apocalyptic could keep me away from your Christmas dinner, Sinead," Father Patrick confirmed with a smile.

As the Flanagans headed outside into the cold night air and said their farewells, they didn't notice the dark storm front on the horizon.

࿓࿔

Mara woke in the early morning to a completely quiet house. It was a rare enough occasion in the Flanagan household to warrant a moment to just lie there and enjoy it. Debating whether to roll over and go back to sleep or get up, she decided she was too awake to go back to sleep and quietly rolled over to the edge of the bed to find Molly still sleeping on the air mattress below. Turning on her other side, she quietly stood up, careful to avoid the squeaky floorboard next to her bedside table. She softly padded over to the window and carefully lifted the curtain so as not to shine too much light on Molly's face. As she peered through the frosted pane of glass, Mara saw her Christmas wish had been granted: a respectable layer of snow blanketed the surrounding hillside.

"Molly!" she whispered. "Psst! Molly! Come here and look at this!" She could barely keep her voice low enough so as not to wake the rest of the house.

Molly unconsciously pulled the blankets up around her ears, as if trying to get away from Mara's voice, and muttered softly.

"Molly! Wake up! It's been snowing!" she whispered more loudly this time.

Molly sighed. "What?" Her tone was sleepy and annoyed.

"It snowed last night. Come, take a look!"

Molly blearily emerged from her fortress of blankets and joined her at the window. She rubbed sleepily at her eyes, then blinked twice, like she thought she might be dreaming.

"My God, it *did* snow!"

11

"Come on, let's go wake up the boys." Mara grabbed her hand and crossed the hall to Michael's room, where he and Brendan were sleeping soundly.

"Michael. Michael!" she hissed at her brother.

An unintelligible grunt emerged from the darkened room, but neither of the boys stirred.

"Michael! Brendan! Wake up! It's been snowing!"
Still nothing.

"Brendan! Molly's here in her pyjamas," Mara teased, stepping inside her brother's room and sauntering over to the window.

"Mara!" Molly hissed at her, blushing as she folded her arms across her chest.

"Wha-?" Brendan sat up, still half-asleep.

Mara laughed, then pulled the curtain back, flooding the room with sunlight glistening off the snow-covered hills.

"Mara! What the fecking hell?" Michael roared at her, sitting bolt upright in his bed, his tired eyes angrily trying to focus on her.

"Don't you use that kind of language with me, Michael Flanagan," his older sister snapped at him, using the full volume of her voice now.

"I'll say whatever I bloody well like after you've just woken me up!"

"Just you wait until I tell Mam…" Mara snapped back. Michael lunged out of bed in an attempt to grab her but was thwarted by the arrival of their father standing in the doorway. Dermot Flanagan was not a man who was prone to impatience, but both Mara and Michael sensed that they'd gotten to the end of his limits in that moment.

"And what exactly is going on here?"

The room exploded into a cacophony of the Flanagan siblings blaming each other for the noise. Dermot held up a hand to silence them.

"I don't care who woke up whom. It's Christmas morning, we have guests, and we're going to act like the good hosts we are." He turned on his heel and went back to his room, his words final.

Michael threw Mara a dirty look for getting them both into trouble, but she ignored him because her mother called for her.

"Mara! You and Molly meet me in the kitchen, and we'll get breakfast started."

Michael smirked at her, clearly pleased that their parents were annoyed with her.

"And Michael?" their mother's voice rang out.

"What Mam?"

"You and Brendan better be up and dressed in five minutes to help your father with clearing snow. We have guests coming over later."

Mara laughed at him as she went downstairs with Molly, glad to know that she wasn't the only one who'd annoyed their parents. There was a lot of emphatic stomping around as Michael got up and dressed, but he wasn't nearly as snarky to her anymore now that they'd both been punished for their behaviour.

"When are we going to open presents?" Mara asked as she entered the kitchen.

"After church, like always," her mother reminded her. "That way, we can open them with your grandfather."

"Are ye sure there's even going to be church this morning, Mrs. Flanagan?" Molly asked, looking out the window at Dermot, Michael, and Brendan sweeping away the snow from the back stairs to make a path to the shed where they kept the shovels. "I'm not so sure any cars are going to make it up the hill."

"Well, in any case, we should still get a start on

breakfast, just in case." She pulled out the pots and pans from the cupboards, while the girls got out the ingredients from the refrigerator. Noticing that the refrigerator light didn't come on when she opened the door, Mara went over to the light switch by the door and tried it. Nothing happened.

"I think the electricity's out." She flicked the switch again for emphasis.

Molly and Sinead both stopped what they were doing and went to check on the lights in the front room, just in case it was only the kitchen bulb that was out.

"Must've gone out sometime in the night," Molly said, rejoining her.

"Well now, I told you that your Christmas wish was going to bring trouble." Sinead stood there with her hands on her hips, assessing the situation.

"So, we'll have the gas burners to work with, but no oven, which means no turkey…"

"And no pie," Mara finished her sentence. Her shoulders slumped in disappointment. This wasn't turning out to be the magical Christmas she'd hoped for.

"Did someone say, 'no pie'?" Michael asked, standing in the doorway with Brendan.

"Come inside. You're letting all the cold air in," his mother chastised. "And yes, the electricity's gone out, which means no oven to cook the turkey or pie in, but we've still got the burners to work with."

"Great. So, we can have all the veggies we want, but none of the good parts of Christmas dinner." He shot Mara a look that said he blamed her for all this. Just then, the phone rang, making them jump.

"How is that still working if the power is out?" Brendan asked.

"Well, since it's a landline and it's not a cordless

phone, it really only requires the tiniest spark of electricity to work," Molly replied. "It's because of…"

Her voice trailed off when she realized no one was paying attention.

Sinead picked up the phone. "Hello?" After a quick conversation, she hung up.

"Who was that?" Michael asked.

"That was Father Patrick calling to let us know that he's cancelled Mass this morning, on account of the roads."

"So, no church and no Christmas dinner," Michael grumbled.

Sinead's face took on a determined look. "We may not be able to go to church, but we are still going to have Christmas together like we planned." Her tone brooked no argument.

"But, without electricity to cook half the food, how are we going to have dinner? And how exactly are we supposed to get Grandda and Father Patrick here, or did ye forget that you invited them both to dinner today?"

"I haven't forgotten," Sinead replied. She was interrupted by the arrival of her husband.

"Well, the front steps and pathway are cleared, but those roads are something else," Dermot told them.

"Alright, troops! We're going to save Christmas, so it's time to get to work." Sinead stood in front of them like a general in front of her soldiers.

"Dermot and Michael. You two are going to go down to Liam's and get the wheelbarrow ye forgot down there weeks ago."

Michael looked at her sheepishly. He'd been supposed to go, and retrieve said wheelbarrow but had kept forgetting about it, having most likely been distracted by his girlfriend, Eliza Kennedy. Mara thanked her lucky stars that the Kennedys had gone to Limerick this Christmas to visit Eliza's aunt, or else she'd likely have been stuck here, too, and then Mara really would have thought that was the worst Christmas ever.

"What do we need with a wheelbarrow?" Dermot asked.

"We're going to need it to transport the food and the presents down to your father's," Sinead told him, as if this was perfectly obvious. "He's the only one of us with a wood stove."

Dermot nodded, seeing his wife's point.

"Molly and Brendan, you two are going to go up to Father Patrick's and help bring him down to Liam's place."

"I thought the roads were impassable?" Brendan asked.

"By car, maybe. But it's only a short distance from here to the church and you two should be able to navigate them by foot. Just stick close to the fences and you'll be fine," Sinead replied, dismissing his worries.

"Mara, you and I'll stay here and get everything together and ready to take down to your grandfather's. Everybody clear on what they need to do?"

They all nodded, no one wanting to disagree with her.

"Well, then, what are we waiting for? Let's get going!"

೫⊙೧೪

"So, even if we go and get the wheelbarrow, how exactly are we supposed to get it back and forth between Grandda's and ours?" Michael asked.

"What d'ye mean?" Dermot asked, preoccupied

with watching his step as they hugged the fence line that separated the Flanagans' string of cottages and the Byrnes' farm.

Michael took a pebble that had been poking through the snow and tossed it out into the lane, watching as it skittered across the glassy surface.

"Hmmm…" Dermot paused to think. "Well, I'm sure you'll think of something." He looked back and gave his son a cheeky smile.

"Why am I the one who has to come up with a plan?"

"Because you'll be the one wheeling it back and forth," Dermot replied matter-of-factly. Several minutes later, the two of them reached Liam Flanagan's cottage.

"Hello! Da? You here?" Dermot called out as they went inside, kicking the snow off their boots so as not to drag it in with them.

"Of course, I'm here. Where'd ye think I'd get into this weather?" Liam teased his son as he shuffled out into the kitchen from the front room where he'd been waiting for them.

"Good day, Grandda," Michael greeted him. "Happy Christmas, to ye."

"Hmmm," was his grandfather's stony reply. "So, have ye come to tell me that church is cancelled? Because Father Patrick beat you to it. I suppose this means that supper's off, too?" Liam seemed especially upset about this.

"No, Da. We're still having supper," Dermot tried to reassure him.

"There's no electricity," Liam said, speaking over top of him, like he hadn't quite heard his son's response.

"We need to borrow back the wheelbarrow, Grandda," Michael said, changing the subject.

"What are ye saying?" Liam asked, raising his voice.

"We need to borrow back the wheelbarrow, Da."

"What? What d'ye need that for?"

"To put you in it and wheel you up to our place for supper," Michael teased, but kept his voice low, thinking Liam wouldn't hear him.

"You're not putting me in a wheelbarrow!" Liam exclaimed.

"Oh yeah, sure, that you heard." Dermot gave his father an exasperated look.

"I may be old, and I may be hard of hearing, but I'm not so old and feeble to not give you a swift slap upside the head, Dermot Flanagan," his father warned him.

"It wasn't me who suggested it, Da. It was your grandson!" Dermot exclaimed, annoyed at being falsely accused.

Michael chuckled, clearly amused at seeing his father being treated like a child.

"Who I've got a mind to slap upside the head myself."

Michael coughed loudly, his laughter caught in his throat.

"We need the wheelbarrow to bring the food and presents down here," Dermot told his father, speaking loudly and clearly. "We're having dinner down here. You're the only one with a wood stove." He gestured towards the stove, hoping he'd pick up on what he was trying to tell him.

"Well, why don't you have it here? I've got the wood stove," Liam said, over top of him.

Dermot sighed. "Alright, so you go on up to the house and help your mother and sister bring the food down here. I'll stay here with your grandfather and try to make space for everyone and find some candles to light the place."

Michael nodded. "Where d'ye keep the wheelbarrow, Grandda?"

Liam reached out and gave Dermot a light slap on the back of the head.

"What was that for?"

"You said something about the wheelbarrow," Liam replied, emphasizing his point with another little slap.

"*I'm* not the one who said it, Da, and we didn't say anything about putting *you* in it!"

Michael made a beeline for the door, chuckling all the way to the shed as he heard his father and grandfather bickering with one another.

☙❧

Molly shivered a bit as the wind whistled through them on its way down the deserted lane.

"Sure is pretty out," Brendan said from behind her, the two of them forging their path to the churchyard.

"If a tad on the cold side." Molly pulled her coat tighter around her. She hugged the fence line, carefully watching where she stepped. Still, she found an icy patch.

"Oh!"

Brendan reached out and grabbed her by the elbow, steadying her.

"Thanks."

"No problem." He smiled down at her, that same winning smile she loved so much. Even if her Christmas wasn't going exactly how she'd planned, she found that she was perfectly happy so long as she was spending it with him. Several minutes later, they arrived at Father Patrick's, smoke wafting lazily out of the chimney.

"Looks like he's home," Brendan said, approaching the door.

"Hello? Father Patrick?" Molly called out as she and Brendan poked their heads inside the little cottage. Father Patrick turned around in his armchair to look at them.

"Hello, Brendan. Molly," replied, sounding surprised to see them. "What brings you all the way over here?"

"We stayed overnight with the Flanagans," Molly supplied. "Since the roads are still bad, we're spending Christmas with them."

The priest nodded at this wise decision.

"Sinead asked us to come up here and help you down to Liam's place. We're moving dinner down there on account of him having the only wood stove."

"Oh, well, isn't that thoughtful of her? I'd resigned myself to having to miss out on her Christmas dinner this year."

"Well, we're glad to make your day," Molly smiled at him.

"Well, then, I'll just grab my coat and boots and we can head down." The priest hopped up from his chair with a spring in his step and followed the two of them out the door.

ॐ

"Looks like Molly, Brendan, and Father Patrick are here!" Mara called from the front room window.

"Perfect timing. Everything is almost ready." Sinead dusted her hands on the apron around her waist, surveying the make-shift dinner they'd put together.

"Hello!" Brendan called out from the back door,

bringing Molly and the priest in with him.

"Father Patrick! It's so good you were able to make it down," Dermot greeted him, shaking his hand.

"Thanks to these two," he replied, nodding towards Brendan and Molly.

"Well, we couldn't just let a little snow derail Christmas dinner," Sinead replied matter-of-factly.

"And just look at what you've done under the circumstances," Father Patrick praised them all. The table may have been set with mismatching sets of plates and glasses from Liam's cupboards, the room may have been lit with various candles of differing shapes and sizes, and they may have been missing one or two key parts of their dinner, but to everyone assembled, it still seemed perfect.

"Well, let's not just stand here looking at everything. Take your seats and let's get started." Sinead motioned for them all to sit down while she brought over the turkey and placed it at the centre of the table. As Mara took her place beside her grandfather, who was sitting at the head of the table, she noticed how no one looked more eager to tuck into their meal than Liam.

"Before we get started, may I propose a toast?" Father Patrick asked, standing and raising his glass.

"I really wish you wouldn't, Father," Liam mumbled, looking annoyed at the interruption, but everyone ignored him.

"May your days be many and your troubles be few. May all God's blessings descend upon you. May peace be within you, may your heart be strong. May you find what you're seeking wherever you roam. To friends, family, and community. Slàinte!"

"Slàinte!" Liam replied, getting in the last word. "Now, can we eat?"

Mara chuckled. "Yes, Grandda, now we can eat."

She smiled at him, and everyone gathered around her. Everyone who was most important to her was sitting at the table. Even if this Christmas wasn't quite like how she'd thought it would be, she wouldn't have had it any other way.

O'Leary's Pub

O'Leary's Pub had stood at the centre of Ballyclara for going on two-hundred-and-fifty years, and it was more than apt to say that it was the beating heart of the village. Once built as a small inn for travellers passing through from the monastic site at nearby Glendalough, it had stood silent witness to the comings and goings of Ballyclara residents and travellers alike. Everything from the banal and the benign: young couples from opposing religions plotting to run off and get married, and even the occasional highway robbery had been discussed in its wood-panelled booths. Nowadays, it mostly observed weddings and wakes, birthdays and retirement parties, proposals and the odd mild scandal. Occasionally, it still overheard a young couple plotting to run away and get married, but mostly, the pub now enjoyed listening to the daily gossip of its patrons. And the gossip on everyone's lips today was none other than what would become of *O'Leary's* now that its long-time owner, the titular Mr. O'Leary, had passed away peacefully in his sleep at a good, old age.

"A fine day for it," Anna McCaffrey, one of the pub's longest-serving patrons ruefully observed, passing through its doors to escape the deluge outside. For it would seem that Mother Nature herself had keenly felt the passing of the late Mr. O'Leary as much as anyone, and had appropriately expressed her grief with an almost flood-like rain.

"Bad enough to have to bury your husband, but there's something especially awful about having to do it in this weather," Anna's friend, Sinead Flanagan, agreed with her, giving her umbrella a little shake, careful not to spray any droplets on anyone gathered nearby. The pub had been somberly dressed for the wake, and despite the weather, it was nearly full of well-wishers coming to pay their respects to the widow O'Leary.

"I hope it won't be like this when I go," Anna mused, settling herself into her usual booth, the one her grandson's girlfriend, Molly, had been sitting in for nearly thirty minutes, fending off the silent glares of the old biddies hoping to guilt her into giving it up.

Molly looked relieved at the sight of them.

"Surely, that won't be for a long ways off," she said, helping Anna to free an arm from her soggy raincoat.

"This here's our booth, so you can take that look right off your face, Nuala O'Shaughnessy. Move along," Anna barked at one of the women passing by, giving them a disdainful look. Mrs. O'Shaughnessy sniffed at Anna's forthright tone but moved on, eyes searching for an open place to sit, like a hawk looking for prey.

"What's a long ways off?" Brendan, Anna's

grandson asked, joining them, smoothing his funeral suit as he sat down. He was followed by Sinead's son, Michael.

"You know what *won't* be a long way off?" Anna asked, cleverly changing the subject. "A decision about what to do with this pub. Old Mrs. O'Leary'll be getting offers from all over for it now. The two of you shouldn't wait too long before you two put in an offer on it your-selves." Having a vested interest in her grandson's future and the prospect of free drinks for life from her favourite pub, Anna was keen to see her grandson and his best friend become the place's new owners. Everyone knew that Mr. O'Leary had had the two of them in mind to take it over from him, eventually, and to Anna's mind, it just made sense to finalize the transition.

"Gran!" Brendan protested. "Mr. O'Leary's barely in the ground, and here ye are at his own wake trying to sell the pub out from under his widow."

"Come on, now. What's there to dither about? Wouldn't ye like to have a place to put those culinary skills to use, Molly? You've always said how you wanted to run your own pub or restaurant."

"Well, I…" Molly looked liked she would dearly like to be anywhere except trapped between her boy-friend's grandmother and the booth wall.

"And don't ye want to have your financial future secure before the two of ye get married?" Anna rounded on her grandson, non-plussed by Molly's lack of words.

"Gran! I haven't even asked Molly to marry me yet…"

Anna dismissed this comment with an elegant wave of her hand. "Ah, but ye will. Everyone knows it, and don't ye want to make sure that the two of ye have a steady income for when ye do? And what about you, Michael? Eliza Kennedy's not going to wait around forever for you to put together the money for a ring."

Michael Flanagan shifted uncomfortably under Mrs. McCaffrey's stare.

"Do we even know that the pub is officially up for sale?" Molly asked, finding her voice.

"If it's not by the end of the day, it soon will be. It's not like she'll be able to run the place at her age," Anna said with certainty. "And sure, they've no children to take it over. That's why Mr. O'Leary was so keen for the two of ye to take it on before he passed."

"What are we talking about?" Mara, Sinead's daughter asked, joining them.

"Gran's trying to sell the pub for Mrs. O'Leary at her husband's wake," Brendan replied, a little of both shock and amusement in his voice.

"You two won't want to wait long to put in an offer on the place," Maud Drummond butted into conversation, forcing the Flanagans to scooch down until they were all packed into the booth like sardines in a can. Maud, a life-long friend of Anna's since their primary school days, and next-door neighbours throughout the entirety of their adult lives, joined them.

"Ah, ye see! Someone speaking common sense."

"No offense to ye, Maud, but of course she'd agree with ye, Gran. Maud always agrees with ye."

Anna made a motion to hush her grandson. "She does not! And who would know better than Maud whether the two of you should put in an offer on this place than her, what with her Andrew being Mrs. O'Leary's solicitor? Go on, Maud. Ye must have some inside information to share with us about what she plans to do with the place."

Maud, so used to being over-shadowed by her more exuberant friends, Anna, and Riona Byrne, fairly preened at momentarily having the attention of the table.

"Well, as ye know, my Andy would never disclose clients' information, even to his own mother…"

"Yeah, yeah, doctor-patient confidentiality and such," Anna interrupted, motioning for her friend to move on.

"Actually, I think that only applies to doctors, Gran."

"Lawyer-client confidentiality, then," Anna retorted, annoyed at having been interrupted. "Forgive my grandson, Maud. Go on."

Maud waited patiently for half a second to ensure the McCaffreys were done with their bickering before she continued. "As I was saying, my Andy would never talk about a client's personal information. He's a good lad like that, but there has been a rumour that Mrs. O'Leary has a great-nephew over in Kilkenny that's looking to put in an offer."

Anna scoffed at this idea. "I've met the lad once, and that was enough for me to know that I wouldn't trust him to mind sheep, let alone run a pub."

"Still, it means there's interest in the place," Maud pointed out. "And he's not the only one with an offer. Apparently, there's even some big pub chain up in Dublin that's rumoured to be eyeing it, too."

Everyone around the table made various audible noises of derision at this idea.

"That's the last thing we need, some jackeen thinking they know this place better than we do." Michael snorted at the thought.

"Well, that just proves my point." Anna couldn't help but gloat. "Mrs. O'Leary would be a fool to sell this place to anyone but the two of you, so you'd best be getting yourselves together and set up a meeting with her as soon as ye can."

"It's sure coming down out there," Dermot Flanagan, Sinead's husband said, coming over to their booth. He snagged an empty chair from the table nearby and drew himself up to the edge of the table, removing his rain-slicked coat. "What are you all over here doing looking like a den of thieves?"

"Your son and my grandson are going to be proud new owners of *O'Leary's*," Anna crowed.

Brendan tried to get her to keep her voice down, for they'd begun to draw the stares of nearby punters.

"Is that so?" Dermot asked, mildly surprised by the news.

"*McCaffrey and Flanagan.* That has a nice ring to it." Anna stared off like she was envisioning what the gold lettering above the door would look like.

"*Flanagan and McCaffrey,*" Michael corrected. "I think we should go alphabetical."

"You would, because it puts you first," Brendan teased him.

"*Walsh's,*" Molly offered, putting in her own name. "That's what we should call it, since I'll be the one doing all the work in the kitchen, and we all know pubs become famous because of their food."

Everyone around the table considered the name, but none seemed to like it much.

"You'll be a McCaffrey soon enough, dear," Anna told her, patting her on the hand. "So, there's no need to use your maiden name."

Mara, who'd never seen the need to be anything but a Flanagan, rolled her eyes at this. "And what if she doesn't want to change her name?"

Anna blinked at her, like she'd never considered this thought before. "Of course, she'll be a McCaffrey."

"Ok, I think we should maybe put a pin in any

name changes for now," Brendan rushed in, ever the peacemaker. Thankfully for all involved, they were all distracted by the arrival of Mrs. O'Leary fresh from the internment.

"Here she is now," Anna pointed out, taking charge of the situation once more. "Let's go and offer our condolences. And you two," she said, nodding towards Brendan and Michael, "try to work on getting a meeting with her while you're talking to her."

"Yes, Gran, we'll be sure to harass a sweet, old lady on the day of her husband's wake about whether she'll sell his beloved pub to us," Brendan replied, sarcastically, as they moved away from the booth and another group filled their place, leaving the pub to listen in on a new conversation.

𝔰𝔒ℭℜ

Two Weeks Later

O'Leary's Pub may have gone by many names over the years, but it had always sat in the village centre along the banks of the small river running through Ballyclara. It had originally been named *The Wayfarer Inn*, a resting spot for weary travellers moving through the Wicklow Mountains. Then, it was bought by the O'Donoghue family in the nineteenth century, at which time it took the convention of many Irish pubs, taking the name of the family that owned it. It had remained with the O'Donoghues for nearly a century, at which time it was purchased by Mr. O'Leary's great-grandfather, and it had been re-christened once more. The pub was rather fond of its current name; the O'Leary family had treated it well, spending much time and care to keep the modest, two-storey, red-brick building well-maintained.

At one point, it had boasted four small rooms on its top floor, the kitchen and dining area on the ground floor, along with a smoking room for gentlemen patrons. Nowadays, one room upstairs had been turned into an in-door bathroom, and another into a small office. The smoking area had been dismantled sometime in the twentieth century, opening up the dining area to make more room. It wondered what changes its new owners would make.

"Ready?" Brendan asked, standing outside the black-painted front door.

"Nope," Michael replied, shaking his head, his longish, dark hair swaying with the movement.

Brendan looked as if he couldn't blame him; he didn't seem any more ready than Michael did. Even though Anna had had all the confidence in the world that the pub should rightly pass to the two of them, they didn't seem so sure.

"Ready now?"

"No, but if we stand out here any longer, then the whole of Ballyclara's going to wonder if we've gone mad."

"Maybe they won't be so far off," Brendan said quietly under his breath as he reached forward and pushed open the door. A sign on the door stated the pub was closed for the afternoon for a private meeting.

The recently widowed Mrs. O'Leary sat at one of the tables, alone in the empty pub. She'd always been small and frail-looking to the two young men, but she seemed even more so now. The expression on Brendan's face said that he felt terrible coming here so soon after the funeral to discuss business, even if it had been Mrs. O'Leary who'd reached out to them.

"Michael, Brendan, it's yourselves," she greeted

them, pushing her chair back and standing up to welcome them.

"Mrs. O'Leary." Brendan stepped forward and gave her a gentle hug. She felt as frail through her soft cotton cardigan as she looked. "We're so sorry for your loss."

"Thank you, dears." She gave them a small smile. "Why don't you two have a seat while I go and put the kettle on?"

"Oh! We could go and do that, Mrs. O'Leary."

"No, no. Sit yourselves down. Gives these old hands something to do."

She motioned to two of the wooden chairs at the table before shuffling towards the kitchen. The two of them stood there a moment, seemingly unsure of what to do, before Michael made the decision to sit down first, Brendan following his lead. The two of them sat in silence for a moment, the anticipation building. Brendan fiddled nervously with his tie. His thoughts drifted to Molly, who'd given it to him this morning so he could make a good impression.

"Oh wow! I think ye should go and buy a pub every day," she'd said, coming in to assess his new style. "I'm liking this new look, but not loving the tie. Here, try this one."

She'd handed him a long, black box. He'd opened it to reveal a dark blue tie.

"It matches your eyes," she'd said, kissing him on the cheek.

"You shouldn't have."

"Well, it's not every day that your boyfriend buys you a pub."

"Touché."

He touched the tie now, thinking of her and what this business proposal would mean for their futures.

31

"Leave that alone, would ye? You're making me nervous now," Michael hissed peevishly.

Brendan ignored his best friend and continued to adjust the collar of his tie. The longer Mrs. O'Leary made them wait, the more it seemed to feel like a noose.

"I'll do as I please," Brendan snapped at him.

Michael didn't say anything, but he knew from his raised eyebrows that his tone had been sharper than he'd meant it to be.

"Sorry," Brendan muttered softly.

His outburst was surprising for him. He was usually the calm, collected one, but today was an important day, and so much depended on the two of them convincing Mrs. O'Leary to sell her husband's pub to a pair of twenty-somethings without any business degrees between them, and their only experience being that they'd worked here occasionally, and they'd frequented a few pubs in their short lives so far. Nevertheless, this hadn't deterred them, and it was a good thing too: if it was left to anyone else, there was a chance they could tear down the historic pub to make way for some ghastly chain store or something. It wasn't just the history of the pub or its importance to the village that was important to Brendan, though. He had other big plans, and they all rather depended on having the extra income the pub could bring them.

"Well, look at it this way: if we don't convince her, we're no worse off than we were before. We've still got the contracting business," Michael said in a rare moment of optimism, trying to smooth over the outburst.

Michael and Brendan had started their own contracting business straight out of secondary school. They'd both been working on Ballyclara's buildings with their fathers since they were kids, and they figured that now they might as well get paid for it. So, they took their skills and opened their own business together. It was steady work, but it wasn't enough to really do more than put a roof over their heads.

Brendan glanced at him sideways.

"That's all well and good for you, Michael Flanagan, but some of us have to save up to buy Molly a ring, and I'll never make the kind of money I need for the ring she deserves from what we make through contracting."

Michael's eyes went wide with surprise.

"A ring?" he asked after a brief pause. "So, your Gran was right, and you intend on marrying Molly? And when, exactly, were ye planning on telling your best friend about all of this? Sometime before ye made it to the church, I hope?"

Brendan gave him an exasperated look. "Of course, I'd have told ye before then. I was just waiting to get the ring and put some kind of plan together about how I'm going to propose to her first."

"Well, it's about time!" Michael beamed at him.

Brendan smiled back. "What do ye mean?"

"Oh, come off it," Michael scolded him. "Everyone in the whole of Ballyclara has known since we were kids that you'd marry Molly Walsh. It's a wonder it's taken ye this long to pluck up the courage. I was beginning to think ye were going to keep the poor girl waiting forever."

Brendan blushed, as if only now realizing that his love life had been the source of so much gossip.

"So, does that mean I get to be your best man?"

"Of course! I couldn't imagine anyone else standing by my side when I get married." He put a hand on Michael's shoulder and squeezed it.

"Ye know, if you and Molly get engaged, Eliza's going to put loads of pressure on me." Michael's tone was light, but nevertheless, there was some tension in the way he sat perched on the edge of his chair that showed Brendan that this meeting wasn't the only thing worrying him now.

Brendan regarded him with some surprise. "Is there something you want to tell me? Something about you planning to marry Eliza?"

"Oh, I think ye'll have awhile to wait for that." Michael sounded sure on this point.

Brendan's shoulders relaxed a little. Michael's on-again/off-again relationship with Eliza Kennedy had been somewhat of a source of anxiety between the two friends. It wasn't that Brendan didn't want to see his best friend happy; he'd love nothing more than to see Michael settled and happy, but with the right person. In Brendan's opinion, Eliza just wasn't that person. She'd always had ambitions beyond Ballyclara, and none of them involved living a quiet, contented life with the likes of Michael Flanagan.

"Well, it's not like there's any rush, is there?"

Michael smiled at him, relieved.

"Where is Mrs. O'Leary with that tea? Is it just me, or did she go all the way to Belfast for it?" Michael asked, changing the subject.

"Shhh! Keep your voice down. I'm sure she'll be along soon."

"What do you think she'd do if we just snuck out right now?" Michael asked, putting a voice to the very thought Brendan was having.

He shot him a look but didn't have time to respond, as Mrs. O'Leary re-appeared from the kitchen, as if the mere mention of her had conjured her up. She shuffled towards the table, the contents of the tea tray she was carrying rattling slightly with her gait.

"Can I help ye with that, Mrs. O'Leary?" Brendan asked. His chair made a scraping sound across the wooden floor as he jumped from his seat, ready to help out.

"No, no, dears. Sit down," she assured them, placing the tray carefully on the table before them. "Tea?"

They both nodded, more to be polite than for anything else. They were anxious to get this meeting started. Nevertheless, they patiently watched as she poured the tea into their white ceramic cups and handed them to them. Brendan took a small sip before gently placing it on the table beside him, sitting up in his chair, ready to begin.

Mrs. O'Leary settled herself across from them. "Mighty fine of ye to come to the funeral. Mr. O'Leary would have been thrilled to have ye there."

"Of course," Brendan replied, "Twas nothing at all. Shame about his passing."

"A fine funeral, it was," Michael chimed in.

Brendan glanced at him sideways, and Michael shrugged.

"What?"

Brendan rolled his eyes at him and muttered something under his breath. Michael rolled his eyes right back at him.

"Ye know what I meant."

"I never know what you mean. Just let me do the talking from here on out, alright?"

Thankfully, Mrs. O'Leary, whose hearing was failing in her old age, didn't catch any of this exchange.

Eager to get this meeting started, Brendan turned his attention back to the matter at hand. "Mrs. O'Leary, as ye know, Michael and I wanted to talk to you about…"

She held up an aged hand to stop him. "I know why the two of ye are here. I am the one who invited you both, after all. You two want to buy this pub from me."

She looked around the room wistfully. Brendan and Michael both nodded, understanding that she had more to say.

"Before ye begin with your proposal, I feel it's only right that you both should know that yours is not the only offer I've heard this week."

They nodded, only a hint of trepidation mirrored in each other's expression. "Yes, of course. We might've heard something to that effect."

"One of my sister's grandsons and his wife have expressed an interest in the place. You know, to keep it in the family."

They both nodded. Anna had told them as much at the wake.

"And there's been another offer, as well."

Both men tried to look calm about this news.

"There's a pub in Dublin...Well, a whole chain of them, really. Anyways, they're also interested in expanding here in Ballyclara."

Brendan and Michael's already shaky confidence was wavering even more. They might be able to compete with the likes of her great-nephew, but competing against a big chain? That was well outside of their budget.

"You two aren't afraid of a little competition, are ye?"

"Nah, Mrs. O'Leary. We're not worried. We're still interested in buying the pub, if you're still interested in hearing our proposal," Michael boasted with more confidence than either he or Brendan felt.

"Excellent. I hope ye don't mind, but I've invited my solicitor, Mr. Drummond, to sit with us today. I've no mind for business; that was always Mr. O'Leary's area. He should be here any moment, now."

As if summoned by the wind, the door opened to admit Andrew Drummond.

"Hello! Am I late? The kids were dragging their feet

about going to school this morning."

"No, dear, we're just getting started. Come and sit down. Have some tea."

Michael and Brendan rose from their seats to shake hands with Andrew. "Hello, Andrew."

"Brendan! Michael. Nice to see you both," he said, taking a seat on the same side of the table as Mrs. O'Leary.

"Have a seat, have a seat," Mrs. O'Leary gestured to them. "Can I pour ye some tea, Andrew?"

"No, that's alright, Mrs. O'Leary, I'm fine. So, where are we in the presentation?"

"I was just informing the lads about the other offers that I've received so far."

"Ah yes." Andrew set his black leather briefcase on the table and opened it up, pulling out a folded piece of paper. "Here are the other offers that we've received so far."

Taking the paper and opening it up, Brendan and Michael tried to keep their faces neutral as they read the offers from the other buyers, but Brendan couldn't help the creases that formed on his forehead as his eyes widened.

There's no way we can afford to compete with this. Brendan glanced sideways at Michael and could see the same thought in his deep blue eyes.

Should we pack it in right now? those same blue eyes asked.

Brendan paused for half a second and gave it some serious thought. He shook his head. They'd made a commitment to themselves and their families that they were going to buy this place, and not fighting for that dream now would be a betrayal to themselves. There was also the fact that he didn't want to go home to Molly as the guy who didn't try at something because he was afraid of failing. They needed to go through with this to the bitter end, no matter the outcome. Michael nodded. He'd support whatever decision Brendan made; that was just the kind of best friend he was.

Taking a breath, Brendan and Michael began to lay out their proposal, all the vision they had for her husband's pub. At the end of their speech, Brendan handed Andrew a document. "Here's everything all written up, in case you'd like to take a look at it in more detail."

He took a shaky breath, glad that the hard part was over with.

"Well, gentleman, thank you for all of this. Is there anything you'd like to add?"

Brendan took a moment before speaking again. "I'd just like to say one thing. Mrs. O'Leary, as you know, both Michael and I've been coming to *O'Leary's* since, well, let's just say, since we were probably a little too young to be in here." Brendan gave her a sly smile. "We both want to assure you that we want nothing more than to keep the vision your husband had for his family's pub the same as it's always been. We don't want to come in and take away the character and the love that has been put into these walls over the last two hundred and fifty years. We know we can't give you the same offers as the others on that list, but what we can promise to do is keep what's special about *O'Leary's* and carry it into the future."

Mrs. O'Leary smiled at them both. "Thank you, lads, for coming in today. You've given me plenty to think about. I'll need some time to think over these proposals and then I'll get back to ye."

"Thank you for your time, Mrs. O'Leary." Michael and Brendan rose from their seats and shook hands, making their way home, feeling buoyed by the sense of pride and relief that comes after accomplishing something that was really important to them. But if they thought presenting their proposal was going to be the hard part of all this, they were about to find out that they were sorely mistaken.

೫೦ഌ

It had been the longest, most torturous eight days and ten hours of Brendan's life waiting for Mrs. O'Leary's response. And it wasn't just him and Michael who felt it; the entire village had been on tenterhooks waiting to find out who the new owners were going to be. They'd been filling the pub every night since Michael and Brendan's meeting in the hopes of being there when the final news was delivered.

"You're fidgeting," Molly chastised him as she calmly sipped from her pint.

"It has to mean it's a no, right?" he asked. "That's why it's taking so long for her to get back to us about it. It's a no."

"It means that she hasn't made up her mind yet. It's a big decision, and she has a right to take as long as she needs to make it."

"But it's been over a week now…"

"And it could be another three weeks, for all we know. Fidgeting and worrying about it won't make a difference."

"Jaysus, I hope not. And how can you be so calm about all this? This is a huge decision for you, too. You'll finally get to have your dream of running your own kitchen. So why am I the only one who's going mad with all this waiting?"

"Well…" Molly was cut off by the arrival of Michael and Mara Flanagan slipping into their booth.

"Let me guess, he's totally freaking out, isn't he?" Mara asked, interrupting their conversation. "This one's been pacing the floors at Mam and Da's place all morning."

"Have not!" Michael retorted, but it was more out of a habit of arguing with his older sister.

"Have to," his mother interrupted, joining the conversation with her husband and Anna McCaffrey.

"What are you all doing here?" Brendan asked, looking around the assembled group.

"Your gran has declared that today's the day that Mrs. O'Leary will give us her decision, and so here we are," Mara replied.

"What makes ye so sure that today's the day she'll decide?" he asked his grandmother. This was the third time that she'd been "sure" that Mrs. O'Leary was going to get back to them.

"I overheard it from Maud Drummond who was talking to Una Kennedy, who said she heard it from…"

"I just need the highlights, Gran," Brendan cut her off before she launched into another long-winded story that no doubt involved every old gossip in the whole village.

Anna seemed a bit put out by this impertinence, but nevertheless got to her point. "In any case, it seems that Mrs. O'Leary has come to a decision about the pub, so I'm sure you'll be hearing from her today, and we all should be right here to hear it."

"Well, we're going to need more drinks, then," Molly said, rising from the booth to head towards the bar.

"I'll help," Mara followed her.

With very little to do but wait for this announcement his grandmother was sure would come, Brendan started drumming his fingers on the table again.

"Would ye stop that? You're making me nervous

all over again."

Brendan gave Michael a sympathetic look and stopped, if for no other reason than to stop him from complaining. They'd all just settled into their silence when Andrew Drummond approached their table.

"Andrew! How's yourself?" Anna greeted him. She could barely keep the excitement out of her voice.

"I'm well, Mrs. McCaffrey, and yourself?"

"I'd be much better if you're here to tell us the good news that Brendan and Michael are the new owners of this pub."

Andrew dipped his head and smiled. "Well, as ye know, I'm not the one who gets to make that decision, but I'm here to escort Brendan and Michael to the woman who can. She's upstairs in the office, lads. What d'ye say?"

Brendan gave Michael a nervous look. "Ready?"

"No, but it's time we got our answer." The both of them rose from the booth.

"What's this?" Molly asked, returning with their drinks. "Do we know something?"

"We're about to find out."

"Oh! Well, in that case, good luck." She gave him a quick kiss on the cheek.

"Thanks, love." Brendan followed Michael towards the stairs. Before beginning the climb to the second storey, he turned back one more time to look at Molly, who gave him a thumbs up sign.

"Mrs. O'Leary! How are ye this fine day?" he greeted her a moment later, entering her office.

"I'm well, lads, thanks for asking. So, take a seat." She motioned towards the seats in front of her husband's old desk. The small office was still cluttered from all of Mr. O'Leary's old files and boxes.

"I'm sorry for making ye wait so long. I wanted to

make sure I weighed all my options. I hope I didn't cause ye too much trouble."

Brendan and Michael tried to assuage her, even though they'd both been more than a little anxious over the last week.

"Well, I won't make ye wait any longer. I've finally come to a decision about selling the pub, and I wanted the both of you to be the first to know."

Brendan took in a deep breath, bracing himself for disappointment.

ဆာ၈

Several minutes later, Brendan and Michael descended the stairs to the pub, fully aware that every eye in the place was trained on them as they walked calmly to the booth where their family was waiting.

"Well?" Molly finally asked after several seconds of silence, anticipation in her voice. "What did she say?"

Brendan looked at Michael, who nodded. "You're looking at the proud new owners of *O'Leary's Pub*!"

And with that, the residents of Ballyclara, and the pub, relaxed, knowing that their beloved communal gathering space could not be in better hands.

The Proposal

"Well, what do ye think?" Brendan held out the black velvet engagement ring box for his best friend, Michael Flanagan, to look at.

"What are you asking him for? Michael doesn't know the first thing about engagement rings. Have you forgotten how long Eliza Kennedy's been waiting for hers?" Mara Flanagan, Michael's sister, asked.

"Cute, sis. That's real gas, that is," Michael retorted as his sister smirked at him.

"Oh, look at that! It's gorgeous! Molly's going to love it," Mara exclaimed, ignoring her younger brother.

"And Brendan should take your word because?" her brother asked. "It's not like you've been married, or even engaged, for that matter."

Brendan and Mara both shot him a dirty look.

43

"Because she's my best friend and I think I know a little something about the kind of engagement ring she'd like, considering that we happen to talk about these things. Some of the stereotypes about girls happen to be right, ye know." Mara tossed the towel she'd been using to wipe down the pint glasses over her shoulder and put her hands on her hips, challenging her brother to make another smart-ass comment.

"Eejit!" Brendan hissed at him, giving him a gentle slap on the back of the head.

"Ouch!" Michael complained. "I'm sorry, sis. You're right. I thought we were doing a bit, and I took it too far."

Mara didn't reply, but looked less like she wanted to kill him.

"Here, Brendan. Let me take a look at that," Jack O'Shaughnessy, one of their regular punters, said, breaking up the little argument brewing between the Flanagan siblings. "I've been married going on forty years now to my Nuala, so I'd say I know a thing or two about choosing the right kind of ring."

Brendan carefully handed over the small box like it was the most precious object in the world. Jack put on his glasses, inspecting the ring up close.

"Fair play to ye, Brendan. That's a real beauty, that is. Mara's right. Molly'll love it." He handed the box back with as much care as it had been given to him.

"See?" Mara pointed to Jack, emphasizing her point. "Now, put it away before she comes out of the kitchen again and spots ye flashing it around."

Brendan snapped the box shut, tucking it safely into his pocket. This was their first week as owners of *O'Leary's Pub*, and Molly had burst in and out of the kitchen every few minutes in the last hour to exclaim about some exciting new idea she'd about recipes and new kitchen appliances she wanted to buy.

"Do ye have a plan for proposing to her?"

"Well, I was hoping the two of ye might help me with that," he said, pointing to the Flanagan siblings.

Michael and Mara looked at him, intrigued.

"I was hoping that ye might hold the fort down here for me tomorrow night."

"Shouldn't be a problem," Michael replied. They hadn't officially re-opened the place since taking over its management, so things were a bit slow as the villagers waited for the big re-opening at the end of the week. "Mondays are slow days, anyways."

"And what do ye need from me?" Mara asked. "To help him around here?"

"Actually, I was hoping you could take Molly out for a girls' day, get her out of the house for me."

Mara mulled this over, then nodded. "I can do that. And what are you going to be doing in the meantime?"

"I'm going to be cooking her favourite meal and doing the house up nice, so when she comes home from her girls' day, the place will be all romantic."

Mara looked at him with appreciation. "I think that's sweet. She'll like that."

"Let's hope so," Brendan replied, a note of anxiety in his voice. Just then, the door to the kitchen opened.

"Right on time," Mara teased.

"You know what this kitchen needs? A banana slicer."

"A banana slicer? What on earth for? Don't ye have a perfectly good set of chef's knives in there for chopping and slicing and whatever else ye need? And more to the point, we don't even have anything on the menu with bananas, love," Brendan tried to reason with her.

"Yeah, but that's why we should get one. Then that way we'll have a need to put bananas on the menu. Oooh! I just had an idea for a new recipe…" An excited look came over Molly's face and she headed back to the kitchen. Halfway there, she paused and turned around. "Wait, what exactly are you four plotting?"

"Nothing!" the Flanagans replied at the same time as Brendan said, "I don't know what ye mean, love."

Molly looked unconvinced.

"When I came out here, just now, you four looked like you were plotting something. Jack? What are you all up to?"

"Sorry, Molly, but I'm just a simple man sitting here, quietly drinking his pint."

"Right." Her tone was skeptical as she turned around to head back into the kitchen.

Brendan breathed a sigh of relief when the door swung shut behind her.

"Well, if she wasn't suspicious before, I think she might be now," Michael said, stating the obvious. "You best get that proposal done, and quickly."

⁜⁝

The next day…

Molly and Brendan were just finishing up their breakfast when she heard a knock on the front door. "Who could that be at this time of the morning?"

Brendan simply shrugged his shoulders and took another sip of his tea, but Molly suspected he was feigning.

"I see you trying to be coy, Brendan McCaffrey, and you're not very good at it." She carried the dirty dishes to the sink before heading over to the door. Standing on her doorstep was her best friend, Mara Flanagan.

"It's a bit early in the morning for ye, isn't it?"

"Now, is that any way to greet your best friend?" Mara asked, handing her a coffee thermos and linked arms with her as they walked inside. "Good day to ye, Brendan. Do ye hear the cheek on this one? You'd think she wasn't happy to see me at all."

"Good morning, Mara." Brendan rose from his chair to give her a hug. "But she has a bit of a point. You're not exactly a functional human being until at least ten in the morning, and it's only just past eight."

Mara shot him a dark look.

Molly sipped her coffee. "I'm not saying I'm not happy to see ye. I'm just wondering that brings you 'round. And why do I have a suspicious feeling that this has something to do with what you all were whispering about last night at the pub?"

"Us?" they chorused together.

"Whatever could ye mean?" Mara asked, playing innocent.

Molly looked at them both suspiciously. "Now I know for sure you're up to something."

"Well, I don't know about Brendan, but I'm here to whisk you away to Dublin for a girls' day out."

"A girls' day out? Ye must be joking. We've a million and one things to do for the re-opening this weekend."

"That's exactly why we need a day off! There's been so much anticipation about whether Mrs. O'Leary would sell the pub to Michael and Brendan, and then we've been working on the re-opening the last week, and I think it's time we took a day just for ourselves."

Molly gave her a skeptical look.

"Oh, come on! You can't tell me you're not just a

little excited to take some time off."

"That's besides the point." Molly crossed her arms across her chest. "I have menus to plan, recipes to tweak, grocery orders to make."

"And all of those things will still be there tomorrow. Come on, I have these coupons for this spa up in Dublin that Eliza's aunt or something gave to her, and, in typical Eliza fashion, she'd rather be dead than caught using coupons, so I said I'd take them off her. I figured her loss, our gain. They expire soon, so let's not let them go to waste."

Molly couldn't deny that the idea of going on a spa day sounded like it would be amazing right now. She felt she should turn down the offer, but between Mara being a single mum and running her own business and Molly investing so much time at the pub lately, it was like they were both always exhausted and barely had any time for each other. Molly was having a hard time remembering when they'd last hung out together.

"What about the renovations? I know we said we weren't going to change much around the pub, but there's still stuff that needs fixing up, a fresh coat of paint..."

"And Brendan and Michael are more than capable of doing those things on their own for a day. They are contractors, after all." Mara put her hands on her hips, showing she wasn't going to take no for an answer.

"Ok, fine," Molly relented.

Mara beamed at her.

"Excellent! Well, that sounds like my cue to head out. You two have a lovely day." Brendan leaned down and kissed her on the cheek.

"I see you, Brendan McCaffrey, and don't think this means that you're off the hook. I still know you're up to something and I'll get whatever plan you're scheming out of ye before the day's done, just you wait and see. And don't forget to complete that list of things that need doing down at the pub that I gave ye earlier!" she shouted at his retreating back.

"Yes, yes," he could be heard saying, turning the corner of the house towards the pub.

"Oh! I should just catch up with him and tell him to do…"

"He'll be fine," Mara said, putting her hands on Molly's shoulders and turning her in the direction of the car. "Now, come along and spend the day with me before you come up with more excuses. I have the whole thing planned. First, I have appointments for us at the spa for hair, make-up, and nails, and then we'll hit up the shopping mall…"

Molly sighed but let Mara gently guide her towards the car and off to their girls' day adventure.

❧❦

A few hours later, Molly and Mara emerged from the spa feeling like entirely different women.

"That was wonderful," Molly sighed, feeling totally relaxed as she breathed in the fresh air. "Thank ye, Mara. I needed that."

"My pleasure! I mean, my motives weren't entirely unselfish. I needed this as much as you did." She grinned at her.

"I'm starving. Are you starving?" Molly changed the subject. "C'mon, let's find somewhere to eat."

"Yeah, all that self-care certainly works up an appetite, doesn't it?" Mara followed her down the street, passing several shops before coming across an Italian place.

"Hey, how about this place? This looks good to you?"

"This'll do," Molly replied, surprising her. Being a chef, Molly was quite choosy about where she liked to eat out. Mara had been on many a trip with her where it had taken upwards of an hour for her to finally settle on a place that would meet her standards.

"People just don't know the difference between good food and *great* food," she'd always say when Mara would complain that she was being too picky. So, for her to agree on a place in under ten minutes was quite the achievement.

"Are you sure you're ok with this place?" she asked now, wanting to make sure she wasn't imagining things.

"Sure," she shrugged. "I'm starving and, I mean, how bad can it be?"

₧₧₧

Later that night...

After their day out, Molly and Mara finally arrived back in Ballyclara.

"Oh, wow! I should get moving and get supper together," Molly exclaimed, noticing the late hour.

"I don't think ye need to hurry. It doesn't look like anyone's at home." Mara nodded toward Molly and Brendan's thatched-roof cottage. The house was dark.

"Brendan and Michael must still be working late at the pub," Molly replied, observing the seemingly empty house. "Well, they'll both be hungry when they're done. I'll talk to ye tomorrow?"

"Sure thing."

Molly turned back to give Mara a little wave as she drove off. She walked up the front path and turned her key in the lock to find the living room dimly lit with candles, pink rose petals scattered on the hardwood floor. On the table in front of her was a hand-written note from Brendan.

Meet me in the dining room.

"What's this?" Molly asked, smiling to herself, and headed towards the dining room. A fresh linen tablecloth adorned the table, along with two silver candlesticks and the nice china.

"What have we here?" she asked, admiring the romantic gesture.

"I thought that I'd surprise ye," Brendan said, standing in the kitchen door, his arms crossed casually across his chest, a big smile on his face.

"Well, consider your mission accomplished, then. But what's this all for? Did I forget a special anniversary or something?"

"No, no, nothing like that. Mara was right earlier. You've had to put up with me stressing out over buying the pub, and then all the craziness of learning to run the place. I thought you deserved to have something nice done for you to say thank you for putting up with me." He came over to her and kissed her lightly.

"Who knew you were such a romantic, Brendan McCaffrey?" she said, smiling up at him, then kissed him back. "Just promise me one thing."

"Ok."

"Promise me you did not try and cook for us tonight."

He rolled his eyes at her. "I may not be the chef in this family, but I'm not entirely useless in the kitchen, ye know. I do know my way around a few recipes."

Molly had a hesitant look on her face.

"Oh, come on. It's not that bad. It's just a simple spag bol. Now, come on and sit down. I'm hungry."

He took her hand and led her to the table, holding out her chair for her to sit down. As she settled herself in, her stomach made a most disconcerting flip-flop motion and gurgled slightly.

Oh no, ye don't, she mentally told her stomach. *You are* not *going to ruin this lovely evening Brendan has planned for us.*

It was also in that moment that she'd regretted choosing the first available restaurant instead of being a little more discerning. But she'd been starving at the time, and the Italian place had looked pretty safe. Obviously, she should've listened to her common sense and found a different restaurant.

Another gurgle confirmed this assumption.

Just hold things together through dinner, she bargained with her stomach, hoping it would listen to her.

Brendan emerged a few seconds later with warmed plates of spaghetti bolognese and placed one in front of her. "I know, there's far more glamourous recipes I could've made, but I thought I'd better go with something safer."

She smiled reassuringly at him, breathed in the delicious scent of the pasta, and tried to look enthusiastic. Her stomach, however, was in no mood to cooperate. A pensive look came across her face.

"Oh, come on. Just try it. It's not *that* bad, is it?" Brendan asked, his face looking a tad hurt.

Molly tried to make herself take a bite, but knew she could not go through with it.

"Just one second." She then stood up abruptly and fled from the table in the direction of the bathroom. She never even had a chance to see the black velvet box Brendan had just placed on the table.

༄༅༈

The next day…

"So, how'd it go last night?" Michael asked, nudging Brendan playfully in the ribs. "Did she like the whole romantic dinner by candlelight?"

"It didn't," Brendan replied, wiping a tired hand across his face. Between staying up all night with Molly and getting here early to begin work on the pub, he was exhausted.

Michael's brow furrowed in confusion. "Ye don't mean to say that she turned ye down, did she?"

"What? No." Brendan wiped down the bar. "I never even got to ask the question."

"Lost your nerve, did ye?" Michael teased him, but his expression turned serious as he saw Brendan's face. "Because ye know she loves ye, right? Though God knows what she sees in ye."

Brendan punched him playfully on the arm.

"No, I did not lose my nerve, and yes, I know she loves me. Apparently, it was food poisoning from the place she and Mara had lunch at. She didn't even get a bite of the spag bol in before she was in the bathroom the whole night. I didn't think that proposing on the bathroom floor was exactly the romantic story we wanted to tell our grandchildren, so I held off."

"Ah, shame that. Must've been some real bad food they ate."

"Ugh, don't even talk to me about food," Mara

said, entering the pub, still looking pale around the edges.

"You look like ye had about as much fun last night as Molly did," Brendan told her sympathetically.

"Oh, no! Don't tell me she also ended up with food poisoning?" Mara's shoulders slumped in disappointment.

'Fraid so."

"So, I take it ye didn't get to propose to her, then? I mean, I kind of thought if ye had, that my phone would have been ringing off the hook, but since I was in the bathroom all night, I wasn't exactly checking it."

"Yeah, the timing just wasn't right."

"But you're not going to give up, are ye?" Mara asked, a hint of concern in her voice.

"Of course not! Molly Walsh will be my wife, no matter what. I've just got to come up with a new plan, is all." Brendan sounded determined.

A silence descended upon the three of them.

"Why don't ye take her up to the falls? It's a beautiful spot to propose to someone."

"But that's your spot." The waterfall in the old growth forest just outside of Ballyclara had always been Michael's thinking spot since they were children, the place he'd always run off to when the world just seemed too much. Even though Brendan knew he was welcome there any time, he'd always felt that it was much more Michael's spot than anyone else's.

"I thought maybe you might want to save it for when you propose to Eliza. Whenever that may be," he added, acknowledging their prior conversations about Michael being in no rush to get married anytime soon.

Mara snorted. "And when was the last time that ye saw Eliza Kennedy traipsing through the woods to go up to the falls? I'm fairly certain that proposing to her up there is an excellent way to get her to say no. Hey! Maybe you should try that, then, Michael."

Her brother glared at her.

"You could do up a nice picnic and take the scenic route through the old forest," Michael interrupted, ignoring his sister's comment.

Brendan mulled it over. "Ye know, that's not a bad plan. Thanks, Michael. You've just given me an idea. Say, the two of you wouldn't mind looking after this place tomorrow afternoon, would ye?"

"Of course not, mate," Michael reassured him, patting him on the back. "Don't worry; we'll get the two of ye engaged yet."

ℰℭ

The next day…

"Where are we going?" Molly asked, carefully navigating her way around a fallen, moss-covered tree.

"You'll just have to wait and see," Brendan said from a few feet in front of her, just as he'd been saying since they'd left the pub earlier. All he'd told her was they were going on a picnic, but not where or why. He turned back to give her a coy smile and Molly frowned at him, but he could tell that she was more curious than furious with him as he helped her over a large boulder, slick from the creek flowing beside their path. Light rippled through the old-growth trees, dappling them in green and gold.

"Wait, a second! I know where we are." Molly paused atop the boulder, surveying her surroundings. "It's been a long time since I've been up this way, but we're going to have our picnic by the falls, aren't we?"

"Maybe," Brendan replied, trying to be coy.

She smiled at him, seemingly pleased with the idea.

The two of them continued up the path until they could hear the falls in the distance. A few steps more, and they reached the edge of the meadow. The grass rippled lightly in the breeze, the spray from the waterfall gently splashing into the pool below it. Brendan took her hand and led Molly forward, choosing a spot near the pool. He laid out the blanket he had brought with them and watched as Molly unpacked the contents of the picnic basket.

"What do we have here?" she asked, opening the container and giving it a light sniff. She was still a little wary of food she hadn't prepared herself since her bout of food poisoning.

"That's for dessert," he chastised her, watching as she stuck her finger into the boiled icing of the cake he'd made earlier. She giggled, holding the container away from him so he couldn't take it away from her, but eventually set it down to see what else he'd brought.

"Oh, yum. Prosciutto, arugula, and shaved parmesan sandwiches. And prosecco, and cake! What did I do to deserve all this? Dinner earlier this week, and now this picnic… Are ye sure I didn't forget a special anniversary?"

"No reason," Brendan said around a mouthful of sandwich. "I just wanted to have some time alone with ye, is all. We've been working so hard at the pub lately that I thought it would be nice to spend an afternoon alone with ye."

Molly leaned forward and kissed him lightly.

He thought that this might be his moment and laid his sandwich down on the blanket, about to reach into his pocket for the ring, when they heard the snapping of twigs from the other side of the waterfall. They both looked up, curious to see what animal had interrupted the moment, only to find that it wasn't an animal at all, but a couple of teenagers.

"Do ye think they realize we're here?" Brendan asked, watching the teenagers as they fervently made out with each other. He did his best not to glare at them, but he couldn't help but feel a slight bit of resentment towards them for ruining yet another engagement plan.

"I'd say definitely not," Molly chuckled, trying to discreetly direct her gaze elsewhere as the couple began to remove some of their clothes. "Shall we?"

She got to her feet and began hurriedly packing up their picnic.

"I could just go and…" Brendan started, intending to scare off the young couple.

"Don't ye dare, Brendan McCaffrey!" she hissed at him. "Leave them be. You remember what it was like when we were that age, trying to find a moment to be together without the entire village watching us? Stop being such an old man!"

Brendan grumbled under his breath but helped pack up the rest of their things and picked up the picnic basket. "I'm fairly certain that I was never that awkward of a kisser," he said, glancing over his shoulder at the young couple.

"Wouldn't you like to think so," Molly snorted.

"Are you accusing me of being a terrible kisser, Molly Walsh?" Brendan asked, surprised by this new revelation.

"All I'm saying is that, at fifteen, you were as awkward a kisser as any other fifteen-year-old boy."

"Had a lot of experience kissing other fifteen-year-old boys, did ye then? And here I thought I was your only boyfriend."

Molly shot him an annoyed look. "You were, and you know it! All I'm saying is that ye kissed exactly like how

Erin Bowlen

I imagined every other fifteen-year-old kissed. Now, let's get out of here before they see us, and before we see too much of them."

She took his hand and led him quietly from the meadow, leaving the teenaged couple to their privacy.

ෆ⦚ඛ

Mara was outside working on some of the flower beds in front of the pub when she noticed Molly and Brendan returning from their picnic.

"Back so soon?" she asked, brushing the potting soil off her gloves as she noticed Molly's empty ring finger. "I thought the two of ye had taken the afternoon off?"

She raised an eyebrow in Brendan's direction, and he shook his head. Her shoulders drooped a bit in disappointment.

"We were, but then our lunch got cut short by a couple of teenagers who were, uh, let's just say they were looking for some alone time," Molly explained.

"Oh," Mara said, understanding what she was getting at.

"So, we came back early."

Mara followed the two of them inside, where Michael was polishing glasses behind the bar. He looked like he was about to ask them a question, so Mara quickly gestured behind Molly's back to stop before he got started.

"What's this about rowdy teenagers?" Michael asked instead, following the three of them into the kitchen.

"Oh, just a young couple who'd gone up to the falls to make out," Molly replied, setting out the food for a new recipe she was trying out tonight. "They were so busy trying to kiss each other's faces off they didn't even notice we

58

were there. Brendan wanted to chase them off."

Michael snorted. "I had no idea what an old curmudgeon ye were, mate," he teased. "And you all complain that *I'm* the one who's a grumpy old man."

"Because you are," the three of them chorused. Michael ignored them.

"What's so wrong with wanting to spend some alone time with my girlfriend?" Brendan grumbled.

"Nothing, and I'm sure that teenaged boy would've been asking the same thing if you'd tried to chase them off."

Brendan chuckled. "That would've been a sight."

The others laughed along with him.

"C'mon, old man. I need some help with polishing these glasses before our guests arrive." Michael patted his shoulder and led his friend back out into the pub.

Molly took out some green peppers and began chopping them, their sharp tang filling Mara's nostrils.

"So, up until the teenagers arrived, how was your picnic?"

"It was really nice." A smile crept across Molly's face. "It was a really sweet gesture. I just wish we could've finished our date."

"Oooh." Mara nudged her with her elbow as she grabbed some tomatoes and began slicing them.

"Not like that." Molly rolled her eyes. "Ye know, though, for a moment there, I could've sworn that Brendan was going to propose to me. Right before those kids showed up."

"Oh?" Mara tried to keep her tone neutral, trying not to betray Brendan's plan.

"Yeah, there we were sitting on the grass just having a good time, and suddenly he got this look in his eyes like he... I don't know...."

"Oh, don't leave me hanging. What happened next?"

"Nothing. The kids showed up and we packed up and left."

Mara mentally cursed the teenagers who had chosen today of all days to make the falls their new make out spot.

"Brendan just seems to be trying to get me alone a lot this week. There was the dinner the other night after the spa day…"

"Don't even talk to me about that Italian spot," Mara interrupted. "I don't even want to look at another spag bol for at least a year."

Molly gave her a sympathetic look. "And then there's the picnic today…It just made me think of how long we've been together, and how we're at that point in our lives when marriage seems to be the next step, right? Or am I going mad?"

"I don't think you're going mad," she chose her words carefully.

Molly looked at her inquisitively. "Mara, is there something I don't know?"

Mara felt her stomach twist into a knot. She and Molly never lied to one another, and she didn't want to start now, but she also didn't want to ruin the surprise Brendan had planned, either.

"I'm sure there's loads of things I know you don't," she teased, trying to make her tone playful.

Molly glared at her.

"I just mean that it's obvious the two of ye belong together," Mara replied quickly, her words tumbling out in a rush. "It'd be about time that he should propose to ye."

Molly stared at her for another moment and Mara wondered if she would press the matter further, but she turned back to her food preparations. She breathed a silent breath of relief and prayed that nothing further would prevent Brendan from proposing to Molly. She didn't know how much longer she was going to be able to keep this secret.

ഇറെ

A few days later...

It was the morning of the grand re-opening and Brendan woke with a feeling of anticipation in his stomach. He was *finally* going to propose to Molly today, no matter who or what tried to get in his way this time. He was going to make her a big breakfast to celebrate the pub's re-opening, and then propose to her. Nothing was going to ruin this moment for them.

He rolled over to find Molly still asleep beside him, gently curled on her side. He paused for a moment to watch her chest rise and fall with every breath.

"Did no one tell ye it's creepy to watch someone while they're sleeping, Brendan McCaffrey?"

"Jaysus! I thought ye were still asleep." He put his hand to his chest, feeling his heart racing.

"I've been awake now for awhile. I was just waiting for you to wake up."

"Well, now that you've scared the life out of me, I am."

Molly chuckled to herself as she unfurled her limbs into a long, cat-like stretch, and sighed.

"You stay here. I'm going to make you breakfast in bed."

"You are?" Molly asked, her tone skeptical. "Well,

61

I'm not sure what you'll make, considering that neither of us has had the time to do the shopping."

Brendan sighed, trying to remember when they'd last picked up anything from the store. "Right."

"There might be some bread in the pantry, if you want to make yourself some toast."

Toast. Well, it wasn't exactly the celebratory meal he'd had in mind, but he would make do with what he had.

He rose from the bed and headed downstairs to the kitchen, his bare feet padding softly across the floorboards. He rooted around the kitchen, hoping to find something that resembled a special breakfast, but Molly had been right: all they had was half a loaf of bread. He took out a couple of slices and popped them into the toaster. A few minutes later, Brendan settled himself at the table and lightly buttered his toast. Just as he was about to take his first bite, he heard the back door open.

"Mornin'," Michael greeted him, sitting down beside him. "Cheers, mate."

Michael snatched the piece of toast from Brendan's hand and took a bite. Brendan simply rolled his eyes at him.

"Good morning, Michael. How are you this morning?" he asked, his tone only slightly annoyed. "Come and sit down. Help yourself to my breakfast."

"Fine. Cheers." Michael licked the butter off his fingers.

"So, what brings you 'round?"

"It's our big day," Michael replied, as if it were obvious. "I wanted to spend it with my two best mates. Also, I wanted to know when you're going to finally propose to Molly!"

"I was planning to do it this morning, if you must know. I was planning on making her breakfast in bed, but in all the planning for the opening, we forgot to get groceries. And then you showed up. And keep your voice down; she'll be down any minute."

"She can't hear us…"

"Good morning, Michael. How's yerself?" Molly greeted him as she came into the kitchen. Michael nearly jumped out of the skin at her arrival.

"Well, and yourself, Molly?" he asked, trying not to choke on his piece of toast.

"Would ye like some breakfast? We've nothing in the house, but I thought maybe we could all go down to the pub and I could fix us up something."

"Cheers, Moll. That'd be great."

Brendan rolled his eyes. "Michael's fine. He just ate my toast and he was just telling me how he had loads of thing he'd like to get done today before we open, right Michael?"

"Well, actually I could…"

"That sounds grand, Michael. Thanks for stopping by." Brendan stood up, practically hauling Michael to his feet and shoving him out the back door from whence he came.

With Michael now out of the way, he turned back to Molly, only to find she was no longer there. He walked through to the front room, where he found her putting on her shoes.

"And where are you going?"

"Over to Mara's. She texted to say she'd make breakfast for me so we can go over some things for the opening. I'll see ye down at the pub later." She gave him a quick kiss on the cheek and breezed out the door.

Brendan sighed and sat himself down at the kitchen table, munching on the half-eaten piece of toast Michel had left for him.

"At this rate, I'm going to die a bachelor," he

muttered to himself.

That evening, Brendan was all dressed to go down to the pub for his big night. After checking himself in the mirror, he patted his pocket for the millionth time to check that the ring was still in his pocket. Having rallied himself after this morning's botched attempt to propose, he was more determined than ever to propose to her tonight.

A few hours later, the pub was full, the music loud and joyous, the air warm from the press of all the bodies around them. Michael and Brendan had been run off their feet since the moment they'd opened, trying to keep up with the orders coming through, as were Molly and Mara in the kitchen. They'd even had to recruit Michael's parents, Dermot and Sinead, to help out.

"Love what you've done with the place, lads!" one of the punters said to Brendan, handing him a few bob for his pint. As the night went on and the dancing had begun, Brendan took a moment to catch his breath.

"Go on and dance with her!" Dermot shouted over the din, nodding in Molly's direction. He glanced at the dancefloor and saw that Molly had been coaxed out of the kitchen to enjoy some of the celebrations.

When Brendan didn't move, Dermot gave him a little shove towards the dancefloor. He put his hands in his pockets, searching for the ring he'd been keeping safe all this time, its solid presence having become a comfort to him, a reassurance that one day he *would* marry Molly Walsh. Except the ring was not there. A sense of panic took over him as he patted his pockets, searching for it.

"Looking for this?" Michael asked him, handing

him the ring. "Ye set it down near the bar when he took your keys out of your pocket earlier. Now, go on and propose to her before ye lose it or your nerve!"

Brendan took a step forward and signaled to the band to stop the music. As the musicians stopped playing, everyone looked up, confused. Brendan took a deep breath and steadied himself. He was afraid that Michael might be right: if he didn't do this now, he might never do it. Getting down on one knee in front of Molly, he took out the ring and held it up to her. Audible gasps and excited whispers went through the surrounding crowd, but he was focused on the only person who mattered.

"Molly Walsh, will ye marry me?" Brendan blurted out. It was certainly not the speech he'd been planning on giving, the one he'd been practicing in his mind all week, but he was afraid if he'd didn't get right to the point, something else would belay him.

Molly looked stunned at the gesture and didn't say anything for the longest half a second of Brendan's life, before her face burst into a wide smile.

"Well, it's about time!" she exclaimed, laughter ringing out around them. "I thought ye were going to make me wait until we were old and grey."

Brendan couldn't help but smile in return. "If ye only knew the lengths I've gone to try and get this ring to ye…"

"Is that what all the fuss over the dinner and the picnic were about?"

"And breakfast this morning."

"I *knew* something was up! Didn't I tell you so, Mara?"

"Yes, ye did," Mara agreed.

"Wait, did you know about this the whole time? How many of you were in on this?"

The Flanagan siblings looked at her sheepishly.

"Are ye going to make me stay down here forever?" Brendan interrupted, bringing her attention back to him.

"Oh, you've waited this long. What's a little longer?" Brendan gave her a slight look of desperation.

"Yes, Brendan McCaffrey. I'll marry ye." Her response was almost drowned out by the cheers that went up from the rest of the crowd.

Brendan rose from his knees, took Molly by the waist, and pulled her into a deep kiss, eliciting more cheers.

"Now, let's take a look at this ring," she said, a little breathlessly. Brendan took the ring and tried to slip it onto her ring finger, but it wouldn't quite go on.

"No, no. This can't be happening…"

"It's ok!" Molly tried to reassure him. "We can get it re-sized."

"Promise me you're not going to see this as some kind of sign or something," Brendan groaned.

Molly smiled at him. "Of course not. Nothing's going to stand in the way of you and I getting married, or I'm going to be having quite the conversation with the man upstairs, and he's not going to like how that conversation goes." She winked at him. "Now, put that ring on my pinkie finger. I'm after gettin' engaged, and I don't mean for anything else to get in the way of that!"

Brendan complied with his new fiancée's wishes.

"Well, I think this deserves a toast!" Michael shouted, popping the top off the top of a champagne bottle.

"To Brendan and Molly!" he toasted.

"To Brendan and Molly!" the whole pub chorused and raised their glasses.

The Affair

Eliza Kennedy was used to being disliked.

In fact, she couldn't remember a time when she'd been especially liked by anyone. Sure, she was loved by her parents and her fiancé, Michael Flanagan, but it wasn't the same as being liked for who she was. And now, she wasn't even sure she still had Michael, not after what she did.

If Eliza had ever had a best friend, it probably would've been Michael, even if he wouldn't say the same of her. They'd always been an unusual pairing, she supposed. Michael was from a respected, long-established Ballyclara family, while Eliza's parents had been newcomers to the village, setting up their guest cottage business after seeing the potential of the real estate in the area. The Flanagans made enough to make ends meet, while her family was one of the richest in the village. This should've been

Erin Bowlen

enough to keep them socially divided, but Ballyclara, being as small as it was, it wasn't like there were many other children her age to play with. By the time they'd hit puberty, having few other options, they'd started dating and everyone had just resigned themselves to the idea that they'd end up together.

Michael had always been good to her, but deep down, their whole time together Eliza had always wondered: did he like her for her? Or did he like her because she was pretty, and their relationship was convenient? How could she be sure he wanted her for her, and not just because he didn't have a better option?

Perhaps it was all of these little insecurities weighing her down which had led her to knock on the door of Cottage #103 the day she set her whole world on fire.

෩෧ඞ

It was the end of tourist season, and the number of people flocking to nearby Glendalough had dwindled. Soon, Eliza's parents would be packing up their guest cottage business for the season. Despite her protests, Eliza's mother, Una Kennedy, had commandeered her into working the front desk for the final week. She suspected that this was simply a way for her mother to keep an eye on her. While Una had never been an especially attentive mother, all summer long she'd been finding excuses to keep her close. It had been a tough year for Eliza: earlier in the year, she'd suffered her second miscarriage, and as such, her relationship with Michael had become strained. She knew they were headed for a make-or-break moment, one that they probably should've had much earlier, but that they'd been putting off now.

Eliza was trying not to think about this as she was scrolling through her social media feed when she was interrupted by the chime of the bell above the front door.

"Hey there," a familiar English-accented voice greeted her.

Eliza looked up from behind the computer screen to gaze into the eyes of a man in his mid-twenties, dressed in a plain, grey business suit.

"Well, hello there, Mr. Smith. Back again for more research?"

He smirked at her. "Yeah, I can't seem to get enough of those ruins over in Glendalough."

She gave him a teasing smile. They both knew that Tom Smith hadn't come here for the ruins. Things may have started off that way, but after their first meeting, it had become clear to both of them that there was an attraction.

"Well, you're in luck. It's the last week before we shut things down for the season. You have the whole place to yourself."

She felt a touch of longing at the idea that this was probably the last time she'd see him, the end of their affair.

"Well, maybe you could keep me company," he said, winking scandalously at her, making her forget her worries. She glanced over her shoulder, making sure they were alone.

"Let me just get your room key, and if you'd like to follow me, I'll show you to your cottage."

As they walked down the little gravel path towards the guest cottages, she glanced around, always on the lookout for any busybodies who might be watching them.

"And here you are." She opened the door for

him, ushering him inside. Each of the cottages were identical: small, two-room cottages that included the bedroom and ensuite bathroom. A door at the back of the room opened into the walled-in rose garden that connected to the main house, Rosehill Cottage.

"What excellent service, Miss Kennedy." He pulled her in for a quick kiss.

"Not right now," she warned him. "Give me twenty minutes, then call for the front desk saying you'll be staying an extra night. My mother will want to send over a second set of fresh towels for you, and then we can be alone." She smiled lasciviously at him.

"Well, then. See you in twenty minutes." He reluctantly let her go.

She didn't know what it was about him. There was nothing especially noteworthy or interesting about Tom, but she had a spring in her step the entire way back to the front desk.

ஓ�ରଓ

Ten minutes later, like clockwork, her mother had returned from a meeting in Cork and caught Eliza daydreaming about Mr. Smith.

"Eliza, could you at least pretend to look a little more interested in your work?" her mother asked her.

"Hmm?" She yanked herself away from her daydream, straightening her posture and trying to refocus herself.

Her mother looked at her, unimpressed. "Did we have any guests check in while I was out?"

"Yes! Yes, we did," Eliza replied quickly, uncharacteristically enthusiastic for her.

70

Her mother gave her a curious look.

"Mr. Smith again. I put him in 103." Eliza tried to return to her usual, slightly bored tone.

"Well, that's lucky for him. He's certainly been popular this season. I hope we'll see him again next year."

Eliza tried to look blasé, but she secretly hoped for the same.

"Why don't you go on into the kitchen and take a lunch break? I can cover the desk for a bit." Her mother ushered her out of her chair and sent her on her way.

Eliza had only been in the kitchen a few minutes when the phone at the front desk rang. She stood by the door, trying to listen in on the conversation. She waited until she heard her mother put down the receiver and walk up the corridor to the large storage closet by the kitchen, before she casually asked, "Was that Mr. Smith?"

"Yes. He called down to say that he'd like to stay an extra night. I guess he wants to make one more trip out to the ruins." She turned towards the cupboard and brought down a fresh set of towels.

"Are those going up to his room?"

"Yes. I'll have Mara bring them up to him later."

"I can take those up for you, Mam." She smoothly took the towels from her mother's hands.

"Are ye sure? Mara will be on shift soon. I can just get her to do it then." It was unusual for Eliza to offer to do anything, especially menial work, and clearly her mother was surprised by the gesture.

"No, that's alright. I don't mind."

"Oh, well, thank you, dear." Her mother gave her a pleasant smile.

"No problem. I was planning to go up to the build site to see Michael later, anyways. I'll drop them off on my way." Eliza smiled cheerfully and headed out the front door.

You shouldn't be here, her mind told her as she arrived outside his cottage. *Just walk away now.*

Her feet wouldn't move. She'd been conflicted over the affair the whole summer. On the one hand, Tom made her feel things she'd never felt when she was with Michael. On the other hand, Michael had always been good to her, and her subconscious was reminding her of this.

Just leave the towels outside by the door and then walk away, she told herself.

Instead, her hand reached out and knocked on the door with more confidence than she felt. There was a slight pause, the space of a breath, before she heard a shuffling inside and the door opened.

He'd changed into simple jeans and a button-up shirt. He still wasn't the handsomest man Eliza had ever met, certainly not as handsome, Michael, but still there was something about him she couldn't deny was attractive. She stepped in closer, drawn in by him. She breathed in the scent of his cologne, letting it fill her nostrils.

"Fresh towels," she said, using their cover story.

"Well, I'm sure we can put those to use." The look he gave her made her blush.

Don't do it. Turn around and walk away now.

Ignoring her subconscious, she slipped inside the room and firmly closed the door behind her.

ໝ

It was bad luck for Eliza that Mara Flanagan, Michael's sister, had shown up early for her shift that day. Her young son, Rory, had been up all night with a cold, which had kept Mara up, too. She didn't like leaving him when he was feeling poorly, and she hoped that if she got all her cleaning done a bit early, Mrs. Kennedy might take pity on her and let her go home a bit earlier than usual, especially given it was the end of the tourist season and they hadn't had a new guest in the last week. It was also bad luck that Mara took a chance that the cottages would be empty and skipped her usual check-in at the front desk to see if any new guests had arrived. If she had, maybe she'd have avoided the dilemma she now found herself in.

She was quietly humming along to the playlist on her iPod, pushing her trolley of cleaning supplies, when something caught her eye in one of the cottage windows. She paused a moment, leaned in for a closer look when she noticed the suitcase on the floor by the bed. It was then she noticed it wasn't just the suitcase in the room, but there were guests as well. And not only were there people in the cottage, but one in particular caught her attention.

"Oh. My. God." She placed her hand over her mouth, not quite believing what she was seeing. Quickly grabbing her trolley, Mara dashed out of sight, hoping beyond hope that she'd been mistaken about what she'd seen, even if she knew it was true: her brother's fiancée was sleeping with another man.

ഒ〇ൽ

A sick feeling had settled into the pit of Mara's stomach. After returning her cleaning trolley to its closet, she'd just started walking, not caring that she'd abandoned her shift. With all the work going on over at the construction site for the Kennedys' new home, she doubted anyone would notice she was missing.

The entire walk home she'd asked herself the same question over and over: had it really been Eliza she'd seen through the window of the guest cottage? Or had her eyes just been playing tricks on her? No matter how much she tried to believe the latter, she knew it wasn't true. She'd seen what she'd seen, and now she knew she had a huge decision on her hands: did she tell her brother that she'd seen his fiancée with another man? Or did she forget what she'd seen and let it go? Even though she'd framed it as a question in her mind, she already knew the answer.

Her mother, Sinead, was in the kitchen, preparing their supper, when she walked in.

"Oh, hello, dear." Sinead looked up at her in surprise. "I wasn't expecting you back so soon. Don't you still have a couple of hours on your shift?"

"I wasn't feeling well." She looked around her, blankly, as if she couldn't quite remember how she'd gotten here.

"You do look a bit peaked." Sinead reached out to touch her forehead. "And you do feel a bit warm. Must've picked up what Rory has."

"I'm fine, Mam, just leave it alone, aye?" Mara pulled back from her mother's cool touch on her skin. She didn't have the words to tell her that her skin was warm because she was flushed from the secret she was keeping.

She instantly regretted her snappish tone. It wasn't her mother's fault. She was taking out her anger and frustration on the wrong person. The truth was, the only thing she wanted to do right now was tell her mother everything, to seek her counsel, but she knew she couldn't do that. If anyone needed to hear this first, it had to be

Michael.

"I'm sorry, Mam. I'm just tired. I think I'm going to go upstairs and lie down for a bit."

She hurried up the stairs and flopped face-down on her bed, pulling her duvet over the top of her head, trying to pretend for just a moment that the rest of the world didn't exist.

℮Ↄ

Mara lay in bed for a little while, listening to the sounds of her parents chatting while her mother put supper on the table. When she was sure her parents had settled around the table, she quietly rose from her bed and snuck down the stairs, careful not to step on any of the squeaky floorboards on her way down. She may not be able to talk to her mother about the situation with Eliza just now, but there was one person she could talk to, one person who wouldn't be able to talk to Michael about it before she was ready to tell him what she knew.

The little church at the end of the lane was empty when she entered. She was grateful; the last thing she needed was anyone overhearing what she had to say and spreading it around Ballyclara before she knew what she wanted to do about it. Father Patrick was sitting in the pew near the front of the church. She quietly approached him, both wanting to talk to him and afraid to unburden herself.

"Could I sit with you, Father?" she asked, quietly.

"Of course, child." Father Patrick made room on the pew for her to sit down next to him.

Mara hesitated a moment. Looking at the priest now, this all seemed much too real, but she plucked up her courage and sat down anyways.

"How can I help ye, child?"

"Father, have you ever seen or heard something you weren't supposed to? Something that you knew would hurt someone you cared about, but you weren't sure if you should tell that person?"

Father Patrick sat there so still and quiet for what seemed like ages that Mara wasn't sure if he'd heard her.

"Yes, I have," he finally replied. His face took on a faraway look, like he was remembering something from his past.

"What did you do, father? Did you tell them, even though you knew it would hurt them? Or did you keep it to yourself?"

He smiled kindly at her. "The question is not what I've done in the past or what I'd do in your situation, but what you can live with?"

Mara nodded, knowing this was true.

"Can you live with carrying this secret all on your own, or can you live with the pain that revealing this secret would cause this person you care for?"

It was Mara's turn to sit there quietly while she ruminated on her decision. What could she live with? She'd always known what she needed to do, she'd just needed to have the courage to go through with it.

"Thank ye, Father. I think I know what I have to do." She rose from the pew.

"You're welcome, child. I wish you peace with your decision."

As she walked out of the church, she knew there would be consequences whichever choice she'd made, but she felt better having a clear path forward.

ഇൗ

Eliza wasn't normally the kind of person to rumi-
nate on the things she'd done in her life. Regrets were a
waste of time, in her opinion. But this deserved some
thought, she felt, lying in bed that night with Michael
snoring softly beside her. Normally, she hated it when he
snored, or made any sound at all, for that matter. She was
a light sleeper, woken easily by the slightest sound or
movement. But tonight, it afforded her the time to think
while knowing for sure that he was still asleep, still bliss-
fully unaware of her infidelity.

It wasn't just one thing that had brought her to
this point. She couldn't blame it solely on the fact that she
and Michael had drifted apart over the last several
months. She also couldn't blame it on her own insecurities about feeling like she'd never been anyone's number
one priority, let alone his number one priority. She
couldn't shift the blame that easily onto others, much as
she might like to. She alone had made the decision to en-
ter that cottage the first time and every time thereafter for
a myriad of reasons that were all too big for her to define
right now.

She rolled over on her side to look at him. She'd
thought it would be difficult keeping up this charade, that
she'd be wracked with the guilt. She felt badly that she'd
continuously hurt him, but there was also an odd sense of
peace and relief, too. She felt like, before this summer,
she'd just been plodding along in life, going round and
round in the same circle over and over. Now, she felt like
maybe, just maybe, she'd found the path she was meant
to be on. Maybe it was just the high from the thrill of the
affair, but there was something about blowing up her

whole life that made sense to her. Now, she just had to make up her mind: with the summer coming to its end, did she pluck up the courage to tell Michael everything and move forward with the uncertain future she might have with Tom, or did she forget it had all happened and stayed the course with Michael? It wasn't as easy as she'd thought, leaving the comfort and safety she knew for someone she'd only just met a few months ago, no matter what he'd made her feel.

She turned over onto her back again and stared up at the ceiling. One way or another, she'd have to learn to live with whichever choice she made.

ॐ

The next day, Mara woke up knowing exactly what she needed to do. Quietly dressing so as not to wake anyone in the house, she crept down the stairs and carefully closed the door behind her. If anyone woke to find her gone, they'd just assume that she'd left for work early.

The village was quiet at this time of the morning; most people were still at home, just getting up and making breakfast before work. The only people out and about were those who were opening up their shops. They smiled and waved to her as she walked by, but she focused only on the road ahead of her.

The whole walk down through the village, she'd been telling herself to just forget what she'd seen and go about her day like usual. She needed this job, her son needed her to have this job, her parents needed her to have this job. So much depended on her being able to contribute financially to her family. Even so, she knew she couldn't keep this job.

You'll find somewhere else to work, she kept telling herself, even though it wasn't like jobs were growing on trees in Ballyclara. Nevertheless, she continued down the moral path.

Just as she was approaching the front door of Rosehill Cottage, it opened, and Eliza emerged. Mara panicked and dove behind the hedge adorning the path. It was bad enough that she was going to have to face Michael about all this; she didn't think she could face Eliza, too, at least not without wanting to tear the other woman's face off. Eliza was engrossed in a song she had playing on her iPod, so she didn't notice Mara as she passed by.

Mara checked that the coast was clear before she continued up the front path. She turned the doorknob. As usual, Una Kennedy was standing behind her desk, sorting through the mail that had just arrived that morning.

"Oh, Mara! You're early. You're not due to begin your shift for another hour."

"Mrs. Kennedy? There's something I need to talk to ye about."

"Oh? Of course." Perhaps noticing the serious tone of Mara's voice, Mrs. Kennedy stopped sorting through the mail and looked up at her, expectantly.

"I'm sorry, Mrs. Kennedy, but I can't do my shift today," she blurted out, hoping to just get this over and done with. She noticed how Mrs. Kennedy's face drew down in a furrowed and slightly annoyed look at this news.

"In fact, I can't do any of my shifts anymore. I need to hand in my letter of resignation." She handed over the envelope she had in her hands.

Mrs. Kennedy reluctantly took it from her.

"And no, I can't explain any further." The last thing she needed was to have to tell Mrs. Kennedy that she was resigning because she'd found her daughter sleeping with one of their guests.

"Well, this is most unusual and unexpected." Mrs. Kennedy's tone was clipped. Mara couldn't help but notice how annoyed she seemed.

"I know, and I'm sorry for all this. I know I've let you down."

Mrs. Kennedy had the grace not to agree with her.

"Well, I suppose that's that, then. I'm afraid I don't have your cheque ready for this week, what with the short notice and all."

Mara nodded. She'd forgotten that she still needed to collect her pay cheque for this week.

"I can have it for you at the end of the week. You can come back and collect it then."

Mara wasn't looking forward to that, but she would think about that another time. Right now, she wanted nothing more than to just get out of here.

"Once again, I'm so sorry."

Feeling incredibly awkward, Mara decided to just get out of there before Mrs. Kennedy asked any more questions.

ඥ☙☜

"Hey! Mara!" She turned around to see Michael jogging down the lane to catch up with her.

Her shoulders drooped ever-so-slightly at the sound of her brother's voice calling out to her. She wasn't read for this. She'd been successful in avoiding him since yesterday while she'd sorted out what she'd wanted to do, how she wanted to say this to him, and now that he was right here, she didn't feel ready for this at all.

"Hey." She hoped her voice didn't betray the anxiety she felt at seeing him now.

"Hey, what's going on? I was just down at Rosehill and Mrs. Kennedy was saying how you'd quit your job."

Her heart dropped in her chest a bit to see the look of concern on his face.

"Is everything alright?"

"Yeah, of course," she started, trying to sound casual. "Ye know how it is. I was never going to be a maid for Una Kennedy forever. It was always meant to be a temporary thing."

Michael looked confused. "But I thought ye were using the money from it for the landscaping apprenticeship program you're doing?"

"Yeah, well, I can always find another job working somewhere else."

Michael raised an eyebrow in her direction. "What are you and Rory going to do? Ye know that Mam and Da rely on your income to help out with paying the bills, and they do mind him all day for ye."

"Yeah, I know that, Michael. Ye don't need to be on my case about it," she snapped at him.

He held up his hands in a defensive position. "Sorry. I'm just surprised, is all. It's not like you to just up and leave without a good reason like that."

She sighed. She knew he was only being a good brother and here she was keeping this big secret from him, a secret that was going to change everything for him. She was his big sister; she was supposed to protect *him* from all the bad stuff. She hated being the one stuck in this position of having to break his heart like this. Still, she knew it had to come from her. Eliza wasn't going to tell him; Mara was sure of that, and neither would the man she'd slept with, if he even knew about Michael. So, it had to be her, the only other person who knew what had happened.

Mara sighed. "I need to tell ye something, and I know it's going to hurt, and I know you're going to be furious, but I need to tell it to you anyways."

Michael's dark brow furrowed. "Ok."

He unconsciously squared his shoulders, as if preparing to be hit by a blow.

She took a shaky breath, trying to find the right words that had been eluding her. "I quit my job with the Kennedys because I can't work for them anymore, not after what I saw yesterday afternoon."

Michael didn't say anything, perhaps sensing that she needed to get this out without being interrupted.

"When I went into work yesterday, I went to clean out one of the cottages and I saw Eliza with one of the guests. Together."

Michael's blue eyes looked puzzled, still not putting together the clues of what she was saying.

"They were, ye know, together, *together*," she emphasized, making her point. She didn't want to have to describe what she saw in any further detail.

For a moment, the only sound between them was the bleating of the sheep in the Byrnes' pasture behind their parents' cottage. Mara watched as her brother processed this information, his face going through all the emotions from disbelief, to anger and frustration, sadness and heartbreak, and the awful realization that she was telling him the truth.

"What?"

Mara took in a deep breath. She didn't want to

have to repeat what she'd just said.

"No, ye must be mistaken. Ye must've seen someone else who looked like her."

"I know what I saw, Michael." Her voice was quiet. She hated putting her brother through this. "It was Eliza."

"No. You're wrong. I know that you've never liked Eliza, but this, Mara? Really?"

Mara looked at him, shocked. "I am *not* making this up, Michael! How could you even think such a thing?!"

"What else am I supposed to think?" he asked, his voice hoarse with emotion. "You, Brendan, and Molly have never liked her, and you've never once hesitated to let me know that."

She couldn't disagree with him.

"When she and I decided to stay together after the last miscarriage, don't think I didn't notice how you all looked so disappointed."

"Michael." Her voice was soft, but his face had turned hard.

"Ok," she admitted. "I didn't like Eliza. I *don't* like Eliza," she corrected herself. "She's stuck up, and petty, and overall useless, in my opinion. But before this, I would've said that if she makes you happy, then I'm happy. But Michael, this? Can you really forgive her for this?"

"You're wrong about her, and I'm going to prove it. And maybe you should be more worried about whether I'm going to forgive *you* right now for making up stories about my fiancée." He turned on his heel and marched up the lane, back the way he'd come, while Mara stood there feeling like a dagger had been shoved in her heart.

ഇരു

Eliza sat in the rose garden, looking over at Tom's cottage. He'd left earlier that morning. There'd been no promise to see her again next summer, no invitation to join him in London. For him, the summer was over, and so they were over, too. Not wanting to be the only one who made a fool of themselves for thinking this was anything other than a summer fling, Eliza had quietly slipped out to the rose garden, watching through a crack in the wall as he got into his car and drove off, taking her decision about what to do with her future with him.

A sharp, cool breeze blew down from the mountains, sending a chill down her spine, a foreboding sign. It brought with it something else as well: a voice.

"Eliza!"

His voice carried around the garden, sharp and clear. She glanced over at the open kitchen door, his tall frame filling it. She knew from the moment she saw him that he knew.

"Michael."

He stalked over to her, dark and foreboding, but she wasn't afraid. He might yell or shout, or stomp off in anger, but he'd never hurt her, could never hurt her like that. "Eliza, what the hell is going on?"

For a split second, she thought about playing dumb, but she knew that would only delay the inevitable. "What do you want me to say, Michael?"

"I don't know," he admitted. He sat down on the bench, his head in his hands. She had the sudden urge to go to him, to run her fingers through his dark, silky hair, to reassure him that everything would be alright, but she stayed where she was because she couldn't do that. She knew nothing would be alright between them now.

"Mara says that she saw ye down here in the cottage with one of the guests the other day." There was no need to go into any further detail. They both knew what it was that Mara saw her doing.

So, it was Mara. Eliza had wondered how he'd found out who'd seen her with Tom. Of course, she should've known that Michael's sister would've run straight to him with the news. Mara had always hated her, and she never could resist putting Eliza in her place.

"Tell me it isn't true." His voice was so quiet she almost didn't hear him. She wanted to sit down beside him and tell him what he wanted to hear, but it would've been a disservice to them both.

"You wouldn't be here asking the question if you didn't at least think that there was a possibility that it was true."

"Why would you do this to us?" He finally looked up at her, his eyes searching her face for the answers he needed. He was disappointed, for her face was like a blank canvas.

"I don't know." It was the honest answer. Her bit of self-reflection the night before hadn't provided her with the answers either of them was looking for right now.

"Then who would?" Michael asked, rising to his feet, forcing her to look up at him. "Hmm? Tell me. Who?"

He was like a wild cat, coiled and ready to pounce. She couldn't answer him.

"What were you thinking?" he asked, changing tactics.

"I wasn't," she blurted out. "I wasn't thinking

about you, about us, about anything. Is that what you want to hear? Does that make you feel any better?"

He winced, like he'd been struck by an invisible blow.

"Who is he?" he asked, his voice quiet again.

"Do you really want to know?" She glanced at him and could tell that he didn't, but the question would nag at him forever if he didn't. He folded his arms across his chest, displaying his resolve. She sighed.

"No one. Someone." She said that last one quietly, as if to herself. "Tom Smith."

She watched as Michael thought about why he knew the name, then remembered all the times the two of them had been down drinking in the pub after one of Tom's fictitious trips to Glendalough.

"Why him? What was it about him that…?"

"I don't know, Michael…"

"No, you don't get to get off the hook like that…"

"I. DON'T. KNOW!" she yelled at him. "I was bored, I was lonely, I was grieving, I felt isolated, because he noticed me and made me feel good. Is that what you want to hear? Because the truth is that, it's all of those things and so much more that I don't even know." She reached up and brushed away the tears that were running down her cheeks. She looked at them, surprised to find them there.

"So, this is because…what? I don't pay enough attention to you?"

"Yes! And no." She ran her fingers over her smooth brow. "I told you, I don't know." She felt like none of the words were coming out right.

"Then try to explain it to me." His tone was less angry now.

She took a deep breath, steadying herself.

"After…" Her voice caught in her throat. "After the last miscarriage, I felt something between us just broke. You know the odds; most couples don't stay together after losing a child."

He winced.

"You threw yourself into work. And I'm not saying that's wrong. We all have our ways of coping, but it left me feeling so alone."

He didn't look at her, just looked down at the ground between them.

"Maybe…maybe it was to be expected that we'd fall apart," she continued. "Maybe we should have, instead of holding on to whatever this is." A long silence fell over them. "I don't know what else you want me to say, Michael."

He continued to stand there, silently looking at her. Then he did something completely unexpected: he took a step forward and pulled her into his arms. Her body went rigid at first, surprised by the action, but then she relaxed into the familiarity of him, breathing in the scent of cigarette smoke and cologne.

"I'm sorry." His voice was quiet, barely audible.

This was not at all what she'd expected. If anyone should have been apologizing, it should've been her.

"What for?"

"For making you feel like you were alone in your grief." He pulled back from the hug and looked down into her eyes.

"Michael…"

He held up a hand to stop her. "It wasn't right for me to throw myself into work like that, to stay out until all hours, to not come home to you. I…I just didn't know what else to do."

"Can you forgive me?" she asked, surprising herself. She didn't realize until just now how important his forgiveness would be to her. She knew now that losing Michael's trust, his friendship, was the worst possible thing she could've imagined.

"Maybe," he replied, honestly. "One day, perhaps. But not today."

And with that, he turned on his heel and walked away, and she was left standing there with the uncertainty of wondering if the only person who'd ever treated her well would ever forgive her for what she'd done. She supposed that was exactly what she deserved.

Empty Spaces

It was a dark and stormy night, the rain not so much falling from the sky as pummeling the windshield. You could hardly see the hood of the car, let alone the road right in front of you. The windshield wipers were more of a decoration than being of any real use in weather like this. Perhaps picking up on the tension from his parents, Jimmy Connolly whimpered from his car seat.

"Shhh." His mother unbuckled her seatbelt and reached around, taking his right foot in her hand, trying to comfort him the best she could. "We're almost there. We'll be safe and sound in only a few moments."

They were the last words she would say to her son. A second later, their car hydroplaned and swerved over the line into the ditch on the other side of the road, killing both of his parents. The sounds of the "Wheels on the Bus" and the window wipers swishing across the windshield the only sounds echoing throughout the over-turned car.

ᏄᎧᏣᎧᎡ

Eighteen years later…

Jimmy woke with a start, his heart pounding in his chest. He tried to catch his breath, to slow it – and his racing heart – using the breathing exercises his therapist had taught him.

It was the same dream every night, over and over: him as a baby with his parents on the last night he'd seen them alive. Even if he'd been too young to remember the actual events of that night, it hadn't stopped his brain from filling in the blanks with its own version and tor-menting him.

He rubbed a hand over his face, trying to wipe the disturbing dream from his mind. He pulled back the cur-tains of his bedroom window to see the pre-dawn light casting a warm glow over the Wicklow Mountains sur-rounding his aunt's cottage. He glanced back at his bed, but not being keen to return to his dreams, he decided to get an early start to the day. He padded his way into the kitchen, quietly bringing out the pots and pans, and started breakfast. Twenty minutes later, his aunt came out of her room.

"Ah! You sweet boy. You didn't need to make breakfast again." His aunt took the plate he held out to her.

"Well, I figured since I didn't hear you come in until two in the morning, that I'd let you sleep in. Besides,

I don't mind."

He shrugged nonchalantly. The truth was, he felt it was the least he could do for her, given she'd taken him in as a baby after his parents had died and raised him as her own.

"There was a foal that decided it wanted to be born in the wee hours of the morning, again." His aunt stifled a yawn behind a balled-up fist. She was the only veterinarian for miles around, so it seemed she was perpetually on call. "Why is it that animals never want to be born or get sick in the middle of the day when it's a decent hour?" She winked at him.

"That would just be too easy," he teased.

She smiled and sat down with her plate, pouring hot tea into her cup. He grabbed his own plate and joined her at the table.

"So, where will you and the lads be off to today?" she asked, referring to Brendan McCaffrey and Michael Flanagan. They'd brought Jimmy in as a third set of hands to help them out with their contracting business over the past year. It wasn't glamourous work, but it afforded him a little money to help his aunt out with the mortgage payments and save a little on the side for university next year.

"Old Mrs. O'Leary needs some work done on her roof," he replied around a mouthful of bacon and eggs. "And Father Patrick says some of the dry-stone walls around the church have come down in places, so we'll be working on them, too. Then I've got a shift down in the pub later tonight."

His aunt nodded. "Well, plenty to keep you busy and out of trouble, then."

She ruffled his hair like she'd done when he was a kid as she stood up from the table, heading to the refrigerator for some orange juice.

"Hey!"

"Oh, sorry. Did I mess up that perfectly tousled look all you lads go for these days?" she teased him. "I never saw so many lads spending so much time to make their hair look like it was blown about by a strong wind when all they had to do was stand outside for a minute and let Mother Nature do it for them."

He was about to come up with a snappy retort, but he heard the honk of Michael's old truck in the drive.

"Well, that's me." He quickly took a gulp of tea to wash down his breakfast and deposited his plate in the sink with a clatter.

"Alright, have a good day!" his aunt called out to him. "And don't fall off any roofs!"

"No promises!" he yelled back, only half joking. At nineteen, Jimmy was still all gangly legs and arms that he hadn't quite grown into, and he was known to be rather accident prone.

"Good mornin' to ye, Jimmy, lad," Brendan greeted him as he scooted over on the bench seat in the cab of Michael's Ford Thames pickup truck. Michael gave him a silent wave from the driver's seat.

"Good mornin' to ye."

He squeezed himself in beside the other two and closed the door with a firm slam to ensure the old door would latch properly.

"So, where are we off to first?"

ॐ

After they'd finished their work on Mrs. O'Leary's house, Brendan turned to Jimmy. "Doesn't look like we'll make it to the church today. I called 'round to Father

Patrick, and he said it'd be fine for us to start work on those dry-stone walls tomorrow. In the meantime, though, we should go up to Dublin. A shipment's come in on a few things we need restocked."

"Ok." Jimmy put his toolbox in the back of the truck and hopped into the cab.

A couple of hours later, the three of them were heading back to Ballyclara when they discovered their usual route down the coast through Wicklow was jammed due to construction.

"Shit. Looks like we're going to have to take the Old Military Road."

Michael glanced over at Jimmy, gauging how he would take the news. He and Brendan always took the longer route via Wicklow and Bray to Dublin specifically for him to avoid this road, so he wouldn't have to drive by the spot where his parents had been killed.

Jimmy nodded silently, showing he understood the detour.

He'd been on the Old Military Road since the accident, but despite the beautiful views along the spine of the Wicklow Mountains, it always produced extreme anxiety for him. When there was no other choice, he would take it, but it still rattled him. As they approached the last stretch of road before home, Jimmy gripped the side of the car door, the skin of his knuckles showing white.

"Are ye alright, man?" Brendan asked, glancing over at him, a note of concern in his voice. Despite being a good ten years older than him, Michael and Brendan had sort of adopted Jimmy as the little brother they'd never had and had looked out for him ever since.

"Yeah, no worries."

He did his best to unclench his fingers, to slow down his breathing. He'd never been able to drive by this stretch of road where his parents' car had overturned without a deep sense of trepidation. He wasn't sure if there was some subconscious imprint of the accident on his psyche, or if it was just the knowledge that this was the place it had occurred that contributed to his anxiety, or both. There was just something that about the place that seemed sinister after all these years.

The police and EMTs who'd arrived on the scene had said it was a miracle that he'd survived. When they'd found him, the front end of the car had been crushed when it had flipped over, but the back, where he'd been sitting, had miraculously not been affected. The officials on the scene had said this was probably what had kept him alive. His parents hadn't been so lucky; they'd been killed on impact, a small mercy, he supposed.

He was never more relieved than when he reached the valley where Ballyclara lay nestled between the mountains. The three of them finished their journey in silence, finally arriving at Michael's cottage.

"I need to get down to the school to pick up Des for a doctor's appointment in Cork later. You two alright to unload all of this?"

"Sure, and we're fine," Michael waved him off, sending him on his way. "Say hello to my godson for me."

Michael and Jimmy set about unloading the equipment from the back of his truck

"Want me to drive ye home?" Michael asked a few minutes later, as they finished unloading everything.

"Actually, could ye drop me off in the square?" Jimmy unconsciously glanced over at the Byrnes' farm, which abutted the Flanagans' row of cottages, his mind drifting to thoughts of Karen Byrne.

"Sure, and that's no problem," Michael said, lifting

a ladder out of the back of his truck and placed it beside the shed.

The two men rode back into the village in a comfortable silence. He liked that about Michael. He never felt the need to interrupt a good silence with unnecessary conversation. He pulled the truck to a stop across from the Byrnes' café, and Michael gave him a knowing look.

"See ye down in the pub later?"

"Sure thing."

Jimmy got out of the truck, careful to look both ways before crossing the street. As soon as he walked in, he was greeted by a beautiful smile that belonged to none other than Karen Byrne. Jimmy felt all his earlier anxiety dissipate in the warmth of her gaze.

"Good day to ye," she said. "What can I get ye?"

She tucked a long strand of reddish-gold hair behind her ear as she gave him a shy look.

"Just a coffee, thanks."

He fumbled in his pockets for the change and handed it over to her. The brief moment when their hands connected sent a thrill running through him, and he tried not to blush. The two of them had been secretly dating for a few months now and they'd been so careful to try and act normal around one another so as not to give away their secret. Ballyclara was rife with gossip, and the last thing they needed was her mother, Riona, finding out about the two of them. Riona Byrne had many ideas about what was, and what was not, socially appropriate for her daughter, and Jimmy Connolly firmly fell into the "not" category.

"Thanks," Karen smiled at him, and he thought he could detect a hint of a rosy blush in her cheeks, too, before she quickly turned to pour him his coffee.

"Here you go. I'll have a break in about fifteen

minutes," she said, this time a little quieter so she wouldn't be overheard.

He took the mug from her and sat down at one of the empty tables by the window where he could sit and watch her without appearing to be too stalker-ish about it. He sipped slowly at the hot drink, feeling the warmth emanating throughout his body. Fifteen minutes later, he watched as Karen headed for the back of the building and one of the other employees took over the counter from her. Finishing his coffee, he got up from the table and headed outside, looking around to make sure he wasn't seen as he headed around to the back.

"There you are!"

Karen grabbed him by the hand and pulled him around the corner of the building, pulling him down into a kiss.

"Oh, geez!"

She'd nearly knocked him sideways as she'd grabbed him. She may look delicate on the outside, but people who underestimated her strength were left surprised. She pulled back from the kiss. "Hi."

"Hi." He smiled down at her.

"It's been too long!" she exclaimed, leaning her head against his chest.

"I just saw ye yesterday," he teased, but he felt the same way, too. He hated being separated from her, even if only to go to work.

"Yes, but it's still too long."

"I know." He put his arms around her. He never felt safer than when he was holding her. "We only need to wait until September, then we'll both be at uni, and we can be together all the time."

"Yeah? You mean between classes and work, because at least one of us is going to have to work."

He put a gentle finger over her lips, calming her worries. "I'll find a way to make it work."

Everything he'd been doing the last year was to save up money so that he and Karen could go to Trinity College Dublin together. The two of them had already applied for scholarships, bursaries, everything they could think of to give them enough money so they wouldn't have to depend on anyone for money. She'd even taken to working for her mother in the café after school to give them a little extra. With a little luck and some hard work, they were going to make their dreams come true.

He felt something in her posture shift, and he looked down at her.

"Can we find some time to talk soon? Like, tonight or tomorrow?" Her tone was different, worried.

"I've got to work a shift in the pub tonight." Unconsciously, he glanced at his mobile, noticing the time. "Which I need to be getting to soon."

"Ok, what about tomorrow?"

"We've got a job tomorrow over at the church, and then I've got another shift at the pub." He sighed. Karen was right; it seemed impossible for the two of them to find time for each other, lately.

She looked at him, resignedly. "Well, as soon as we can, then."

"Soon," he promised, leaning down to kiss her again. "You should get back."

She nodded, kissed him again quickly, and headed back inside the café. Jimmy didn't know how the two of them were going to make things work right now, but he was going to be damned if he wasn't going to do everything he could to try and make it so.

ଛଡ

The next day

Molly McCaffrey came out the back of the pub, taking out the trash, when she noticed Karen Byrne walking down the path by the river, looking over her shoulder like she wanted to make sure no one was watching her. Molly was about to dismiss it – Molly had seen her sneaking out at lunch hour or during class a couple of times a week, probably to see Jimmy Connolly – but there was something about the way she was behaving today that seemed different.

"Karen?"

The poor girl nearly jumped out of her skin as she drew near.

"Molly?" she asked, looking bewildered. Close up, Molly could see that she'd been crying. Her eyes darted to and fro, like she was looking for an escape.

"What's wrong?" Molly approached her cautiously.

Suddenly, she burst out crying.

"Oh! Shhh. It's ok." Molly gently pulled her into a hug, holding the girl while she sobbed. "Let's get some tea into ye, hmm?"

Molly, like many an Irishwoman before her, was of the firm belief that most things in life could be solved with a cup of tea. She led Karen into the large pub kitchen and sat her down at one of the stainless-steel counters while she went about the business of making them both some tea. A few minutes later, she handed Karen a cup and watched as she quietly sipped away at the warm drink. She'd stopped crying now, but still sniffled every now and then.

"Here." Molly handed her some tissue to blow her nose. Karen looked at her gratefully.

"I suppose you must think I'm a right eejit," she said, delicately blowing her nose.

"Nah, I'd never think that," Molly told her honestly. The two women sipped their tea quietly for a moment.

"So, what's this about, then? Is it something that Jimmy said or did? Because if he's done something…I don't care if Brendan and Michael think of him as a little brother, they're not afraid to gently sort him out if need be."

"No! No, he's not done anything," Karen assured her in a rush. "Or, well, he did, but it wasn't anything that I didn't want, I promise."

Karen then started crying again. Molly looked at her, unsure of what to do. She hadn't grown up with sisters; the closest she'd had to a sister was her best friend, Mara Flanagan, and now Karen. She wasn't sure what she should do in this situation.

"I'm pregnant!" Karen finally blurted out between tears.

"Oh! *Oh!*" Molly replied. Although she tried to keep her expression neutral, she couldn't help her eyebrows from climbing to her forehead.

"Are ye sure?"

Karen nodded. "I took one of those home pregnancy tests the other week, and I just came back from the clinic. The doctor confirmed it."

Molly nodded.

"Mam's going to kill me!" Karen suddenly exclaimed, putting her head in her hands, starting a fresh wave of tears.

"Oh, honey, I'm sure that's not the case."

"Really? Why don't you ask Mara what her experience has been?"

Molly found she couldn't disagree with her assessment. Mara had become pregnant with her son, Rory, by Karen's older brother, Alistair, when she wasn't much older than Karen was now. After he'd found out Mara was pregnant, he'd swanned off to parts unknown. He'd been the apple of his mother's eye, so his disappearance had been particularly devastating for Riona, who forever after forbade her daughter and her husband, Aidan, from ever having contact with Mara or Rory.

Molly tried to make her tone reassuring. "Maybe she'll have mellowed a bit since then."

Karen rolled her eyes at her. Molly knew she was right. The chances of that were slim to none. "In any case, we'll figure things out, I promise. Whatever you decide, Brendan and I are here for you."

Karen gave her a watery smile.

"Have ye told Jimmy about all of this?" Molly asked, trying not to pressure her.

Karen shook her head. "He's been so busy with work. I tried yesterday when he came over to the café, but he's so fixated on saving up enough so we can both go to uni in the fall. I guess that won't be happening now."

Molly reached across the countertop and squeezed her hand. "That decision is entirely up to you," she reminded her.

"What if he doesn't want it?" Karen's voice was soft, scared. "What if he gets mad, or doesn't want me anymore?"

Molly didn't want to dismiss her fears; it was hard to predict how anyone would react in this situation, but she didn't think Jimmy was the sort of person to cut and run like Alistair had one. Truth be told, she didn't think

Karen did either, but the past was clearly weighing on her.

"Well, you'll never know if you don't tell him. And, like I said, no matter what, Brendan and I will be here for you. Whatever decision you make, we won't leave ye, I promise."

Karen reached across and gave Molly a big hug, squeezing her for dear life, like she was afraid to let go.

"Promise?"

"I promise." Molly gently squeezed her back. "Now, let's see about getting that boyfriend of yours over here so you can tell him the good news, hmm?"

~ ∞ ~

Jimmy felt like he was about to fall out of the pub booth. He was going to be a father. He felt a mixture of emotions: joy, euphoria, and the sheer terrifying panic that comes with the realization that you're suddenly responsible for someone other than yourself.

"Jimmy?"

Karen was looking at him with fear in her eyes, searching his face for a clue as to how he was feeling about all of this.

"Hmm? Oh, jaysus, I'm sorry. I'm thrilled, ecstatic! This is the best news!" He didn't have to put on a face or pretend; it was exactly how he felt.

"Really?" Her voice was cautious, still not quite believing him.

"Really." He came around to the other side of the booth and sat down beside her, putting his arm around her, his other hand on her stomach. He couldn't quite believe that this was all real.

"So, you're not mad or anything?"

"Why would I be mad?" he asked, perplexed.

"It's just… we had so many plans for uni in the fall, and with money being tight…"

"Hey, look at me." He gently put a finger under her chin, raising her eyes to his. "If ye want to have this baby, then we'll find a way to make it all work. If ye don't want to have the baby and go to uni in the fall like we planned, or if ye want the baby and want to go to uni next year, whatever the decision, we'll make it all work."

She reached up and kissed him. She laid her head on his shoulder. "I can't believe we're going to be parents."

"Me either," he agreed. "So, ye do want to have the baby, then?"

She nodded.

He smiled down at her. "Well, I think it's about time that I give you this." He reached into his pocket and pulled out a ring box.

"Karen Elizabeth Byrne, will ye marry me?"

"Oh, Jimmy! It's beautiful!" She gazed down at the small diamond ring.

"But wait, I don't want ye to marry me just because we're having a baby," she said, closing the ring box.

"I'm not. I asked my aunt for my mother's ring weeks ago. I was planning to ask ye in September when we moved to Dublin. This just moves the timeline up a bit." He smiled down at her. "I've wanted to marry you, Karen Byrne, since almost the first day we met."

"Almost?" she asked. Her brow furrowed slightly.

"Well, ye know, since we were kids and all, and I thought girls were yucky and annoying back then…"

She gave him a playful shove.

"Boy, do I wish I could go back and tell my younger self how wrong I was about that?" He gazed lovingly at her.

"Well, in that case, yes, I'll marry you, Jimmy Connelly." She opened the ring box and slipped his mother's engagement ring on her finger, admiring it. A perfect fit.

Jimmy smiled down at her and for the briefest of moments, everything felt right in the world. Somehow, he knew it wouldn't last.

ॐ

"Well, that was some day," Brendan said, getting into bed beside her that night.

"Yeah," Molly agreed. "Do ye think the two of them are going to make it?"

"Well, if the way Jimmy looks at Karen is any indication, I'd put good money on it." He kissed her lightly and turned out the bedside lamp. Molly continued to sit there in the dark for a moment.

"You don't think the two of them will try to make a run for it to Scotland or something before they tell their families, do ye?"

Brendan rolled over, turned on the light, and looked up at her. "Well, I hadn't until ye just mentioned it. Why, do ye think they'll make a run for it and try to marry in secret?"

"I don't know…" she replied honestly. "I've just got this feeling…"

Not wanting to leave things to chance, the next morning Molly got in the truck and drove over to Jimmy's place, the feeling that the two of them were going to run away still with her. She didn't necessarily want to stop the two of them from doing what they wanted, but she knew the both of them well enough to know that they'd regret the way they'd done things if they did it like this. As she pulled up to the farm outside the village, she noticed Jimmy's aunt pull up beside her.

"Well, hello there, Molly. And how's yourself?"

"Hey. I'm well, thanks," Molly greeted her. "Are Jimmy and Karen in?"

"I just got home myself, so let's have a look." She turned off the car and headed up the front stairs, opening the door.

"Jimmy? You at home?" she called out. Molly followed her inside, noticing the packed bags by the door and she knew she'd been right: they were planning to run away.

"Jimmy?"

He and Karen emerged from his bedroom, looking like they'd been found out.

"Molly's here to see ye both."

"Hey Molly," he greeted her. "What can we do for ye?"

"I wanted to check in on the both of ye after yesterday," she replied cautiously. She had a feeling they hadn't told his aunt about their situation yet, given the look on their faces.

"What happened yesterday?" she asked, her parental instincts on full alert.

Molly gave the two of them a look, and Jimmy sighed, tacitly admitting the truth. "Auntie, I think you'd better have a seat."

"I think someone had better tell me what's going on," she countered, folding her arms across her chest.

Jimmy hung his head, his hair falling into his eyes. "Karen and I… we're…" He looked to his fiancée for help getting the words.

Tales from Ballyclara

"We're having a baby," Karen finished his sentence. "And we're engaged." She held out her left hand, showing off the ring as proof.

His aunt stared at them for half a second before she smiled. "Congratulations."

Molly could see that the two of them hadn't been expecting this reaction.

"Yeah?" Jimmy asked, cautiously approaching her.

"Come here." She gestured to the both of them, pulling them both into a hug.

"So, you're not upset or anything?" Karen asked her.

"Well, only if the two of ye were planning on running away. That is what those bags by the door were for, right?"

"Yes," Jimmy replied, sheepishly.

"Jimmy Connolly!" his aunt scolded him.

"We weren't sure how everyone would react," he defended himself. "We wanted to be married first so that no one could stop us."

His aunt gave him a sharp look. "Well, it's a good thing, then, that Molly came over here when she did to put a stop to that plan. I'm assuming that's why ye came over here?"

Molly nodded. "I thought they might regret it if they didn't tell you and the Byrnes first."

"And too tight ye were. Now, tell me, Karen, have ye told your parents yet?"

She shocked her head.

"I thought as much. Well, the two of you are always welcome under this roof, but if you're going to stay here, then you need to talk to the Byrnes first. They've a right to hear this news, and they've a right to hear it from

105

the two of you instead of from one of the town gossips."

"You're right," Jimmy sighed, admitting defeat. "We'll tell them."

"Good, no time like the present, right?"

"You mean right now?" Karen asked, astonished.

"The sooner you get it over with, the sooner you'll be able to move forward." She pulled Karen into a reassuring hug. "Now, I have to head back out on a call. I only came back because I'd forgotten my stethoscope. Ah! Here it is!"

She picked it up from the table. "But I'm sure Molly can go over with the two of ye?"

"Of course," Molly instantly replied, wondering what she'd gotten herself into. "Brendan and I can go with them."

Jimmy's aunt smiled at the three of them. "Well then. Like I said, you're always welcome under this roof. We've not got much, but what we have is yours, Karen. Best of luck telling your parents, and I'll be here when you get back if you need to commiserate." And, with that, she headed back out the door.

"I'm not sure I'm ready for this," Karen admitted, placing a protective hand over her stomach.

Molly couldn't disagree with the sentiment.

∞⃝

"It's alright. We're here with ye." Molly reached out and lightly squeezed Karen's shoulder.

"I don't think we should do this." Karen tried to turn around and walk away, but Jimmy reached out and took her hand. It was one thing telling Jimmy's aunt about the baby. They'd been fairly certain she'd support their decision, but now it was time to face the Byrnes.

"We need to tell them." His tone was firm but kind. She thought she could detect just the slightest hint of nerves.

He had every right to be nervous about going into the Byrnes' house. Riona Byrne had already made her dislike of Jimmy known from the moment she'd caught the two of them kissing behind the café one day. She wasn't going to be best pleased when she found out her one and only daughter was now pregnant at eighteen and planning to marry him.

With more than a little trepidation, Karen reached out and rang the doorbell. Somehow, it didn't feel right just walking in when she was fairly certain she wasn't going to be welcome here for much longer.

"Oh, Karen. Did you forget your key?" her mother greeted her. She looked warily at the others. "I didn't realize we were expecting guests."

"Mam, we need to talk." She tried to keep her voice steady, calm, but she couldn't help a tiny waver from slipping in.

"Of course. Come in." Riona looked at them suspiciously. Karen knew her mother hated surprises, and she certainly wasn't going to like this one.

Riona gestured to the chesterfield in the front room. "Please, take a seat. Can I get you all some tea?"

"No, thanks, Mam. Is Da here? He should hear this, too."

"Of course. He's out back. I'll just go call for him."

Karen nodded and waited while her mother went to get her father. It felt like it took a lifetime. Jimmy squeezed her hand, trying to reassure her. Finally, her parents arrived.

"I didn't know we were expecting company," her father greeted her, coming over to kiss her on the cheek.

"Hi Da." She smiled up at him.

"Oh, I have a nice coffee cake in the kitchen that I made this morning. I'll just go and get it."

"Could ye just leave it, Mam? Could you both just have a seat?" She worried that if she didn't say this to them soon, she'd lose her nerve.

"Ok," her mother replied testily, but did as she was asked. They looked at her expectantly.

Karen took a deep breath and dove right on in. "Mam, Da. Jimmy and I are having a baby. And we're getting married," she added, figuring it was best to rip the band-aid off rather than peeling it off slowly.

It wasn't like she'd expected her parents to like the idea of her marrying Jimmy, or the fact that they were pregnant, but she wasn't quite prepared for the kind of hurt that came next. Her mother's face turned an awful shade of puce, a shade she'd only ever seen when her brother had told their mother that Mara was pregnant. Her father looked dumbstruck at the news, his mouth slightly agape, like he couldn't quite process the information.

"Get out of my house," her mother said after what seemed like an age. Her voice was low, her tone threatening.

"Mam, Jimmy's not going anywhere. He's family now." Karen lifted her chin slightly in defiance, daring her mother to contradict her.

"I didn't mean only him," her mother clarified. Riona's eyes were cold, hard.

"Mrs. Byrne, I really think we need to stay calm about this," Brendan interjected.

"And I think you really need to keep out of this,

Brendan McCaffrey. You're just like your grandmother, always poking your nose into other people's business."

Brendan looked like he was going to interject, but Riona ploughed on.

"Well, I won't have our lives become Ballyclara's latest bit of gossip just because you McCaffreys can't stop looking for trouble. I ought to blame you lot and the Flanagans for this. It's you lot that put foolish ideas in his head about going to uni and dating above his station. Just look at Michael and the example he's set, dating Eliza Kennedy. She's too good for the likes of him, and my daughter is too good for the likes of you, Jimmy Connolly."

Riona's eyes were like spears, hoping to impale Jimmy beneath her gaze.

"Well, I hope you're proud of what you've done."

"As a matter of fact, we are proud of both Karen *and* Jimmy." Molly's tone was crisp and clear as she rose from her spot on the chesterfield. "And you should be, too. I'm sure this wasn't exactly how you thought Karen's life would go when she was little, but she's turned out to be a bright and sensible young woman, and if you won't have her in your house, then she'll certainly have a place with us."

Mrs. Byrne looked at her, aghast, shocked into silence.

"Well, I never…" she spluttered, trying to regain her composure. Very few people were brave enough to stand up to the likes of Riona Byrne, and she wasn't used to anyone talking back to her.

"Jimmy, Karen, I think we're done here." Molly gestured for them to follow her out of the house. With a sinking heart, Karen followed the rest of them out, choosing not to look back.

ॐ

"Are ye alright?" he asked her later that night in bed, back at his aunt's place.

"Yes. No," she admitted.

He wrapped his arms around her, holding her tight. It had been awful the way her mother had reacted to their news, and he knew that as much as he might try, there was nothing he could do to take away that hurt for her. He lightly kissed her shoulder.

"I wish there was something I could do."

She turned over onto her back, looking up at him. "You're doing it right now, just being here."

"And you're sure you still want to go ahead and have the baby and get married."

"I've never been more certain in all my life." She pulled him down into a kiss, and he knew that no matter what came their way, the two of them would be ok.

ॐ

Ten Years Later

"Are ye alright, Da?"

Jimmy looked over at his daughter in the passenger seat, seeing the look of concern in her eyes.

"I know you hate this road…"

Her tone was apologetic, and he knew she blamed herself for the detour. If she hadn't needed to get a costume for the upcoming school play, they wouldn't have had to come up to Dublin, and they wouldn't have been stuck in the detour that had forced them to take the Old Military Road home.

Anxiety gripped him, and not just because of where they were. He'd never told her about his parents, not wanting to pass on his childhood trauma to his daughter, but he could see now that his attempts to hide his own fears about this road hadn't been as successful as he'd thought. His daughter had picked up on his fears in that way that all children did, and he knew now that it was time.

He slowed the car and pulled it over to the side of the road, coming to a stop in front of a spectacular view of the Wicklow Mountains. He turned the key in the ignition and got out of the car, coming around to the passenger side and opened the door for her to get out. The two of them leaned against the warm frame of the car and breathed in the fresh mountain scent of the air.

"Molly Mae, I think it's time I told ye about your grandparents."

And so, he opened up to her about what little he remembered of them, about the accident, about why he rarely came down this road. Standing in this spot with his daughter now, near to where the accident took place, the landscape still gripped at him. But the empty spaces of his heart that had been created by his parents' death had been filled by a family of his own, and in those spaces, he'd finally come to some sort of peace with it all.

Tea with Mrs. Byrne

Father Patrick woke just before the dawn of another beautiful early summer day in Ballyclara. As he rose from his bed, the first rays of the sun's light were peeking out from behind the clouds. The scents of the flowers in bloom, the smell of fresh-cut grass, and yes, even the less pleasant but familiar scent of cow and sheep dung from the nearby farms, were heightened by last night's rain and floated in through the open window. Father Patrick breathed it all in, beginning his practice of listing five things he was grateful for that day. He stretched his arms above his head, working out the kinks in his neck and back, his old muscles and joints protesting a little more than they used to, when he remembered that he'd agreed to go to the Byrnes' house for tea after church this afternoon. His shoulders drooped ever so slightly. Although he knew he shouldn't play favourites with his parishioners, he was still like any parent, and there were those among his flock in whose company he enjoyed spending more time with than others. The Byrnes fell into the latter category.

He would want it to be clear that he took no issue with Mr. Byrne. He seemed a reasonable, if forgettable, sort of man. It was difficult to get to know the real man underneath the long shadow cast by his wife, the formidable Mrs. Byrne. And a long shadow she cast, indeed, not only over those in her own household, but over those in the village as well. She placed an especial importance on appearances did Mrs. Byrne. And it was with this in mind that gave Father Patrick pause when remembering that he was to have tea with the Byrnes later that day, because he knew he wasn't being invited over simply for tea. Rumour had spread throughout the village that the Byrnes' daughter, Karen, and her boyfriend, Jimmy Connolly, were soon to be married, and Mrs. Byrne was decidedly against the relationship. She was even more against speculation about the reason why the two of them were getting married so suddenly from spreading around Ballyclara even more than it already had. For, if Ballyclara's biggest gossips were to be believed – and Father Patrick wasn't saying that he did – Mr. and Mrs. Byrne were to become grandparents again.

He sighed and rose from his bed.

Father Patrick liked Karen Byrne. She'd always been a shy girl, quiet, but bright and easy to talk to. She'd always seemed an agreeable young woman, a quality she'd inherited from her father, he supposed. He also liked Jimmy Connolly. He was a good, dependable young man, and anyone with eyes could see that he'd always adored Karen. Father Patrick wasn't looking forward to being in the middle of the Byrnes' family squabble, of being asked to mediate between the two sides. However, he knew that this was seen as one of his roles due to his position as the village priest. More than anything, he supposed, he wasn't looking forward to having to tell Mrs. Byrne that he had no wish to condemn the relationship between Jimmy and her daughter, that the young couple had meant no harm to anyone; they'd simply fallen in love, and he wasn't going to be one of the people in the village who made them feel ashamed of it.

Father Patrick rose from his bed and made himself his usual simple breakfast of tea, a boiled egg, and a piece of toast.

It wasn't that Father Patrick was entirely unsympathetic to Mrs. Byrne. He realized it had to trouble her that both of her children might now have children of their own out of wedlock. Folks in Ballyclara had a long collective memory, and although no one spoke of who Rory Flanagan's father was, everyone in the village knew it was Alistair Byrne.

Father Patrick grumbled something incoherent to himself.

While he might feel that he needed to treat each of his congregation equally, Father Patrick would be hardpressed to admit that he had no particular fondness for Alistair Byrne. He'd always been an errant sort of person at best, and although he knew it wasn't particularly Christian of him to say so, Father Patrick wouldn't be sad if he never saw the likes of Alistair Byrne in the village again.

The whistle of the kettle brought him out of his reverie. Pouring the hot water into a mug and setting some loose-leaf tea into it to steep, Father Patrick brought his breakfast over to the little wooden table.

The one good thing to look forward to with the Byrnes was that he was sure to get a piece of Mrs. Byrne's famous apple tart at tea later today. Temporarily putting aside thoughts of the Byrnes, he tucked into his breakfast. When he'd finished his meal, he tidied away his dishes; he'd always like to keep a clean cottage.

"Cleanliness is next to godliness, and that extends to the home," his mother had used to say to him as a boy. He wasn't sure if it made him any holier or not, but the ritual of cleaning still comforted him, nonetheless. He finished dressing for the day, grabbed his bible, slipped on his loafers, and headed out into the sunny day.

Walking along the short path from his cottage to the church, Father Patrick admired the gorse that grew up along the roadside, watching the little bumblebees buzzing lazily from flower to flower. He liked the yellow shade of the gorse, it being his favourite colour. It was a cheery sort of colour, bright even on the darkest of days, and if that didn't describe Father Patrick down to a tee, then nothing else would.

At the end of the path, he turned and admired the sight of Aldridge Manor in the distance. The old manor house had once been given to the Church so that the resident priest may live there, but it had always seemed too big of a place for him to live alone.

"A house like that should be filled with laughter and a family," he'd told Father Hanlon, Ballyclara's resident priest, before him.

Father Patrick had instead chosen the little, one-bedroom stone cottage on the church grounds for himself, it seeming to be far more suitable to his needs. Aldridge Manor had sat empty now for a great many years. It seemed a sad thought that no family had come along to live in it in all the time he'd been the priest here and he wondered if perhaps he'd been wrong in not taking it for himself. It was such a shame for the place to sit quiet and lonely, just longing to have someone come and fill its rooms with laughter.

Father Patrick turned his eyes away from the house and looked down at his old watch, the one his brother had given to him as a present many years ago. Noticing the time, he turned from the road and headed towards the church, preparing to greet his congregation.

ഇ⊙രു

Aidan Byrne's stomach grumbled at the tasty scent of breakfast cooking in the next room, its delicious aroma wafting into the dining room where he sat reading his morning paper. The savoury fragrance brought back memories of happier days for his family, days when his children had both been young and still at home, of those happy weekends when they would fill the house with the sounds of an argument breaking out over some toy they were fighting over, but also of laughter at something they'd found hilarious. He felt a pang in his heart that both of his children had left home now, neither of them currently on speaking terms with their parents. Petty divisions had driven a wedge between them and his wife, and so he'd become an unfortunate casualty stuck in the no-man's land between them. One would have thought that after everything that had transpired between their son and Mara Flanagan that his wife would've done things differently with their daughter, Karen, and Jimmy Connolly. But, it seemed, his wife was determined to repeat all the same mistakes again, and so their daughter was now living with Jimmy and his aunt, who'd taken him in and raised him from the time he was a baby. Mr. Byrne liked Jimmy; he was a good lad as far as he was concerned, and he seemed to be good to their Karen, which mattered most to him. But he also knew that his wife had other thoughts on the matter, and Mr. Byrne was not the sort to go against her word on any matter.

With his stomach grumbling more loudly, he decided not to ignore it any longer. Mr. Byrne neatly closed and folded his newspaper and placed it on the table. He rose from his seat, the chair silently gliding over the polished wooden floors, and headed into the kitchen to see how much longer breakfast was going to take before it was ready.

When he entered the kitchen, his wife Riona was chopping apples. He spied a homemade pie crust shell sitting on the counter, waiting to be filled.

"What's this for?" he asked.

"You keep yours hands off that," she snapped at him, even though he hadn't made a move towards it. She turned around, brandishing her paring knife. "That apple tart's for Father Patrick's tea after church."

Mr. Byrne nodded, putting his hands up in a gesture of surrender. He remembered now that his wife had mentioned something of that sort the other day when he'd been half-listening to her. His mouth watered in anticipation, and he was filled with a bit of glee knowing that she was making one of her famous apple tarts that had won her first prize in the Ballyclara Spring Fair for five years running. Mr. Byrne was, after all, a simple man driven by the simple pleasures in life, and food was one of those motivations.

"What's for breakfast, then?" he asked, trying to change the subject.

"I've cooked you some eggs, ham, and toast over there." She nodded towards the pans warming on the stove. "Now go and settle yourself in the dining room and I'll bring them in to you as soon as I've finished chopping these apples."

Reluctantly, Mr. Byrne removed himself from the kitchen and went back into the dining room, waiting to be served. His wife brought their breakfast out a few minutes later.

They passed their meal in silence. Or, rather, Mr. Byrne passed his meal in silence while his wife relayed all of Ballyclara's gossip that she'd heard down in the shops the other day. Maud Drummond was complaining about her hip again but refused to go to the doctor for fear that they'd tell her it would need replacing, and she feared the surgery. Mrs. Kennedy's sister was ill again, and she was thinking of sending her daughter, Eliza, to go and spend some time with her. Mr. O'Sullivan wanted to retire, but his son didn't want to take over the business, and he was afraid of some chain store coming in and replacing him. It only took one Tesco to come in and change the entire fabric of the village. Did he not think so?

Mrs. Byrne was always up on the latest comings and goings on in the village; it was a pity that she'd married a man who couldn't have cared less about their neighbours' personal business. Mr. Byrne simply nodded or added a noncommittal grunt when needed and let her finish her announcements uninterrupted.

"Right," his wife said, after they had finished their meal. She picked up their plates and began moving towards the kitchen. "I need to finish making that apple tart before we head out. Go on upstairs and finish getting dressed for church. Oh, but not before you go and make sure those sheep are locked up in the pen properly. Winnie escaped into the front garden yesterday when I came home from the shops. I thought I told you to fix that break in the fence after the storm?"

"Yes, yes," he said, following her into the kitchen. He leaned against the frame of the back door to put on his wellies and headed out towards the sheep pen.

"Well, it had better be done by tomorrow, Aidan Byrne," she called out through the open window. "What'll the neighbours think of us if we have sheep in our front garden all the time?"

He didn't think it would be especially helpful to point out that their only neighbours were the Flanagans, and he didn't think that they much concerned themselves over the likes of her or what her sheep were doing.

"Good morning, ladies," he pleasantly greeted the ewes, who ambled up to the fence upon his arrival. They were always much happier to see him than his wife, the ewes knowing that he was far more likely to sneak them some treats.

"Here you go, then," he said, giving them each an apple slice he'd nicked from the countertop when Riona hadn't been looking and patting them on the heads. They bleated happily at him and came with him to inspect the temporary repair he'd made on the fence the other day after a big thunderstorm had come in and knocked part of the fence down.

"Well, ladies, this simply won't do now, will it?" he said, giving it a once over. He knew he was going to have to replace this section of fencing entirely, but he'd been putting it off. His to-do list had been much smaller when his children had been around. Or at least when Karen had still been around. Alistair had never had any interest in the farm, had never wanted to work with animals. He'd always regarded such work as menial and, like his mother, had seen the work as being beneath him. His sister, on the other hand, had been much more likely to help out when asked, even though Mr. Byrne knew she had no interest in doing the work full-time. Still, she'd been a help, and he could certainly use a second pair of hands right now.

"Well ladies, why don't we just make a nice agreement right now that if you behave yourselves and stay in the pen for the next couple of days, you'll all get some extra apples? Mmm? How does that sound?"

The sheep bleated at him, sniffing around his pockets.

"That especially means you, Winnie," he said, turning to his most forthright ewe, who was standing apart from the rest of the flock. Winnie was a cheeky one with a mind of her own, not content to behave like the others. She liked to stand out, did Winnie. She was also the one who, more often than not, ended up on Mrs. Byrne's bad side. He suspected that this wasn't entirely coincidental. Winnie didn't bleat at him, apparently refusing to commit to anything.

"Alright, then. I'll come and check on you ladies after church." He snuck them the rest of the apple slices from his pocket and turned to head back inside to change for church.

"Mmm, that smells delicious," he said, wandering back into the kitchen twenty minutes later. He'd arrived just in time to watch as his wife brought the tart out of the oven.

"Keep your hands off it," she scolded him once more.

"I wasn't…" he protested, but he knew it was no use.

"Oh yes, you were. After thirty years of marriage, I know you all too well, Aidan Byrne. Now, I don't want to see you near that tart until it's time for tea after church."

"Yes, dear," he grumbled under his breath, which garnered him a particularly stern look from his wife. Withering under her stare, he backed up a step. He'd never been an overly courageous man, and he wasn't about to start being one right now.

"There," she said, placing the tart on the windowsill. "We'll just let that cool down while we're at church, and it will be perfect by the time Father Patrick arrives. Now let's head out, or we'll be late."

Of course, they weren't even close to being late. They'd arrive just at the right moment, like always. His wife planned everything down to the minute so that it always looked to others as if it were entirely effortless. She moved to the front door to put on her shoes and grabbed her purse.

"Come away from there!" she called out from the little foyer. "I'll not have you sneaking any of that tart in before tea, Aidan Byrne!"

"Yes, yes," he muttered once more, giving the tart one last, longing look before reluctantly tearing himself away to go and put on his shoes and coat. He grabbed the keys for the car and the house, and followed his wife outside, not locking the door behind him. What would've been the point? There'd never been a break-in the entire fifty-odd years that he'd lived in Ballyclara.

ꙅꙙꙅ

It had always seemed a silly little thing to Mr. Byrne that his wife insisted on driving to the little parish church down the road every Sunday. Not to mention that it was enormously inconvenient, given that the seventeenth-century church hadn't been built with a car park in mind. And why would they? You could walk from one end of Ballyclara to the other in twenty minutes, and that was if Mother Nature was being particularly disagreeable. And yet, Mrs. Byrne always insisted on arriving precisely ten minutes before the service began. That way the church would be sure to be mostly full, and so her entrance couldn't help but be noticed by everyone. There was also the inescapable fact that most everyone in the village walked to church every Sunday, come rain or shine, and driving there set the Byrnes slightly above the rest because they took the luxury of doing so.

Like clockwork, just as they pulled out onto the long lane that led to the church, he spied the Flanagans walking down the road. He nodded to Dermot and Sinead and their two children, Michael and Mara, who had Mara's young son, Rory, walking between them. His wife tutted as they passed them by; she hadn't spoken to their neighbours since their son Alistair had left Ballyclara for somewhere in England. It was clear to all that she firmly blamed Mara Flanagan for making her beloved son leave, and that she'd never forgive her for it. Mr. Byrne, however, had other thoughts on the matter, and gave one wistful look in the rear-view mirror at the grandson he had never properly gotten to meet. He was snapped back to attention by the sound of his wife's voice as they passed Aldridge Manor on the left.

"I heard that someone's buying the Old Rectory," his wife told him, using the village's name for the big old house.

"Oh?" he asked. It wasn't that he was particularly interested in the who or what about this announcement, but more just a reflexive response to his wife sharing more tidbits of village gossip.

"I heard that Mara Flanagan was telling Maud Drummond down in the pub just the other day how her mother had said that there was an offer made on the house."

"Oh," he said. He was pleased to hear that the house might be bought and lived in once more. It had been sitting empty for years now, and it seemed a shame that such a grand old place should go without someone to live in it. "Did they say who was looking to buy the place?"

His wife paused a moment; he rarely asked any questions when she was relaying village gossip. "I think they said it was a young woman from Dublin. O'Reilly, I think I heard the name was."

He nodded. This made sense; no one in Ballyclara or the surrounding area would have the money to buy the property, let alone have the funds to restore it. Only someone from the city would have that kind of money.

"O'Reilly…you don't suppose it's one of the O'Reillys that owns the pubs, do you?"

His wife thought this over, and he could tell from the gleam in her eye that she was pleased with the thought. The O'Reillys were a well-known family, and ones who certainly had the kind of money to purchase a hundred Aldridge Manors and fix them all up. They were just the kind of family that Mrs. Byrne wouldn't mind being friends with, not at all.

"Now there's a thought," she mused as they passed by the big old house with its once grand gardens. "They're probably looking to use it as a weekend and holiday home. I'll make it a point to ask Anna McCaffrey to talk to her grandson, Brendan, and see what he can find out. You know how all the best information comes through *O'Leary's* first," she said, referring to Ballyclara's only pub, owned by Brendan McCaffrey and his best friend, Michael Flanagan.

The Byrnes arrived precisely ten minutes before the service started, just in time for Mrs. Byrne to make her rounds and greet all the people she considered important. Highest upon this list were Mr. and Mrs. Kennedy, who, along with their daughter, Eliza, were considered to be the preeminent family in Ballyclara. Or, at least, that was according to Mrs. Byrne, who'd been trying to become best friends with Una Kennedy since they were children to raise her own social status.

"Una, dear," his wife greeted Mrs. Kennedy. "I was sorry to hear about your sister. How is she doing?"

"Oh, ye know," Mrs. Kennedy replied noncommittally. Mr. Byrne couldn't help but notice how Una always seemed to have the look of someone who'd been trapped in a shark tank when confronted with his wife. He couldn't say that he necessarily felt much different sometimes. "Our Eliza's planning to head over to Limerick to see her soon."

His wife nodded sympathetically. He was surprised that his wife didn't press any further on the topic of Eliza. Even Mr. Byrne, who liked to keep out of village gossip, had heard the rumours of her on-again, off-again relationship with Michael Flanagan. One wondered whether they happened to be on again or off again this week. Speaking of the Flanagans, Mr. Byrne turned to see that they'd arrived, the usual signal that the service was about to start soon.

"We should take our seats, dear." He put a hand on the small of his wife's back, directing her to their usual pew near the front of the church.

"We'll talk later," she smiled at Mrs. Kennedy as they took their places and let the service begin.

ℴÈË

No one may be able to say for sure where the origin of Murphy's law came from, but no one could deny its truth. And today, Murphy's law had decided to come for Mrs. Byrne.

Who can say, really, how the mind of a sheep works?

Perhaps Winnie had been drawn in by the scent of Mrs. Byrne's apple tart cooling on the kitchen windowsill when the wind had blown the aroma her way. Perhaps she'd simply took a walk and, knowing from her earlier escape, that the break in the fence that Mr. Byrne had never properly fixed was just big enough for her to sneak out. And, once freed from her pen, perhaps it was just a simple coincidence that she'd noticed that the back door to the kitchen had been left slightly ajar by Mr. Byrne who had been in a hurry to get his wife to church on time. Or perhaps Winnie had simply never liked Mrs. Byrne from the get-go and wanted to stick it to the woman who'd never once given her a treat and had decided it was high time to remedy that situation.

ॐ

After the service, Father Patrick greeted each parishioner as they departed for home and their Sunday dinners. His stomach grumbled, reminding him he hadn't eaten since breakfast. He smiled at each parishioner as they left, some small part of him wishing they'd just hurry along a bit faster so he could get tea with the Byrnes over and done with. Then he spotted them, Mr. and Mrs. Byrne, coming his way. He tried to keep the look of panic out of his eyes.

"Lovely service today, Father Patrick."

"Thank you, Mrs. Byrne. Mr. Byrne." He shook hands with them pleasantly.

"Will you still be joining us for tea this afternoon, Father?" Mrs. Byrne asked him.

"Of course," he replied, pushing aside any thoughts of making up a reasonable excuse not to attend, if for no other reason than his good manners wouldn't let him back out of a promise. "I'll join you as soon as I finish up here."

Mr. and Mrs. Byrne nodded and headed back to their car. He could've asked for a lift with them back to their place, but he preferred to walk. After all, it was such a beautiful day that he couldn't say no to a pleasant walk, and it was only such a little way down the road. He went about closing the church doors and dropped his bible back at his cottage before setting off. All too soon, he was standing on the Byrnes' front doorstep.

"Father Patrick, do come in," Mrs. Byrne smiled at him, her breath coming out in a little *whoosh!* as if she'd been hurriedly doing some last-minute cleaning. He wasn't sure what she would've found left to clean; like him, Mrs. Byrne had always kept a tidy home. He'd never once found a speck of dirt or dust in the place. It was almost as if no one lived there, like it was in a permanent state of being staged, like when a house was being sold. Even when Karen and Alistair had been young, the house had never seemed like it had children living in it, no sign of toys or an errant Lego piece on the floor. It was always a little *too* tidy, and it made him slightly uncomfortable.

"Come in and sit down." She ushered him in. "Here, take a seat."

He noticed she ushered him into the chair closest to the fireplace, the chair which took pride of place in the room. He didn't protest, even though he'd have been just as comfortable sitting informally in the kitchen. It would've had a homier feel, like at the Flanagans' place, for instance. He always felt at home with the Flanagans. They had a very lived-in, happy home. There was never an awkwardness with them, perhaps because they reminded him of the type of home he'd grown up in.

"Are you comfortable?" Mrs. Byrne fretted over him, bringing over a blanket to put on his lap, which he tried to say wasn't necessary, given the gorgeous summer weather outside.

"I'm fine, thank you." He wasn't comfortable being fussed over. Mr. Byrne looked at him sympathetically. Father Patrick suspected he knew all too well what it was like to only require the simple things in life and yet have a wife who constantly looked to have more.

"Well, I'll just go and put on a spot of tea, then, shall I?" Mrs. Byrne said, more than asked. "And then we can discuss an important matter I've been wanting to go over with you. Do you take sugar or milk with your tea?"

"Neither for me, thanks." He tried not to sound apprehensive.

"I'll just go and get that for you, then," she replied, smilingly. "I also made one of my famous apple tarts, especially for you. I do hope you've got room for a slice."

"I've been looking forward to it all morning," Father Patrick replied honestly.

Mrs. Byrne smiled at him, pleased by the compliment, and headed off into the kitchen to fetch the tea, leaving him alone with Mr. Byrne. The two men sat in silence for a moment, which suited Father Patrick just fine. Rarely did he find himself at a loss for words with people, but it had always seemed the case that with Mrs. Byrne he couldn't get much of a word in edge-wise, and with Mr. Byrne, he didn't seem to know what to say when given the chance. He thought perhaps that Mr. Byrne felt much the same way about him, and that after living with Mrs. Byrne for so long, Mr. Byrne had lost the conversational art of talking about anything deeper than the weather.

"Nice weather we're having." Mr. Byrne said, predictably.

"Yes, it is," Father Patrick replied.

"Warmer than expected for this time of year."

"Mmhmm." Father Patrick was mulling over whether to bring up Karen, to broach things with Mr. Byrne first, when he was saved by the Flanagans.

"Look here, now. What could Dermot and Michael Flanagan be doing 'round here of a Sunday?" Mr. Byrne asked, looking out the window behind Father Patrick. He craned his neck around and saw the heads of father and son bobbing by the window on their way to the Byrnes' front door. Mr. Byrne rose from his chair and opened the front door before they knocked.

"Well, and isn't this a surprise?" he greeted them genially. "How can I help you two?"

"Actually, it's more how can *we* help *you*, Mr. Byrne," Michael replied. "Brendan mentioned that he'd heard there was a break in your fence from the storm the other night and thought you might need some help with it."

"Yes, it was a big wind, wasn't it?" Mr. Byrne said. "Why don't you just come on in, and we'll go through the back here? You don't mind if I just take a moment to show Dermot and Michael the fence, do you, Father Patrick?"

"Oh hello, Father Patrick!" Dermot greeted him, just noticing him.

"Not at all. In fact, why don't I come out with you," he said, not wishing to be alone in the house where Mrs. Byrne would have a splendid chance to corner him.

It was then they heard the scream coming from the kitchen.

"Dearest?" Mr. Byrne called out. "What is it?"

"Ah!" Mrs. Byrne screamed again. "Ewe!"

"You?" Mr. Byrne asked, a look of confusion and concern passing between him, the Flanagans, and Father Patrick. "You, who?"

"Ewe!" Mrs. Byrne screamed again.

"I know, dear, but who?" her husband asked again.

This time, he, Father Patrick, and the Flanagans walked through the house to the kitchen to see what the fuss was about.

"Ah, *ewe*," Father Patrick clarified, trying his best to stifle a grin, for there was Winnie, bleating a contented greeting at them, standing in the remains of what had once been Mrs. Byrne's apple tart.

"Shoo! Away with you, you beast!" Mrs. Byrne commanded in a shrill tone, waving her checker-patterned dish cloth at the sheep.

Winnie bleated a little less contentedly at her, but Father Patrick could've sworn there was a bit of a gleam in the ewe's eyes before she turned around and let Mrs. Byrne chase her from the kitchen.

"Well, I guess we can't say we've never had a break-in, in Ballyclara anymore now, can we?" Dermot chuckled, making all four men break out into a chorus of laughter as they watched Mrs. Byrne hilariously chasing Winnie around the back garden, trying to wrangle her into the sheep pen.

And from that moment on, the Byrnes became the only family in Ballyclara to ever worry about locking their doors.

The Mystery of the Auburn-Haired Woman

It was a day like any other in Ballyclara: quiet and uneventful. It was just the sort of day that someone with a love for a good mystery hated about living in a sleepy village like Ballyclara. While a good deal of crime shows might feature salacious crimes happening in little villages just like this one, the truth was, most of the time, they were just quiet villages with not much going on.

Such was the plight of Anna McCaffrey, who'd always loved a good mystery. While she might love living in Ballyclara, there were certainly times when she'd wished that life here was just a little more exciting. It wasn't like she wanted a suspicious death or anything; no that was a little *too* exciting for her, but she just wished something, *anything*, would happen that might be a little out of the ordinary.

It was, perhaps, an unusual trait in someone of her advanced years – after all, Anna was a doting grandmother well into the twilight years of her life – but it couldn't be denied that she'd been fascinated by mystery novels since she was a young girl. By the time she was fourteen, she'd read through the entire mystery section of the school's library. Not that, that was saying much; it wasn't like the little village school had had a plethora of books. As an adult, her love of mystery novels hadn't waned; but between looking after a husband and raising children, she hadn't had much opportunity to indulge in her favourite pastime. Perhaps this was why she seemed to put herself right in the middle of her own mystery when one came along.

As she crested the little knoll between the little parish church and the Flanagans' cottage, she noticed a strange car in the drive, and a fancy one at that. Certainly not the kind of car owned by anyone around here. Anna stepped closer to the hedgerow separating the Flanagans' front garden from the road, trying to peer through the curtains of Sinead's front room, but at this distance, not even her thick-rimmed glasses would help her old eyes see who had come a-calling.

Suddenly, the front door opened, and Anna ducked behind the hedgerow.

"And it was a pleasure to meet you as well, Mrs. Flanagan, Mr. Flanagan," a young, auburn-haired woman said. She looked to be in her mid-twenties, a pretty young woman, not someone Anna had seen in Ballyclara before.

"Oh, we don't stand on formality around here; please, call us Sinead and Dermot."

"Thank you both for everything." The young woman headed towards her fancy car and got in.

"You have a safe trip back to the city now, and we'll see you soon!" Sinead called out as the young woman backed out of the drive and sped off towards the main road. Anna plastered herself against the hedgerow, trying to blend in with its scratchy branches to be sure that she wouldn't be seen.

"Well, now," she said to the open country lane when the car was out of view. "That's something." With a bit of a gleam in her eye, a spring in her step, and a whistle on her lips, Anna headed towards the village.

ഇറ്റ

Riona Byrne had always prided herself on knowing all of Ballyclara's comings and goings before everyone else, so it was with great pleasure that Anna stepped into the Byrnes' café to tell her best friend, Maud Drummond, all about her news of this mysterious stranger in full earshot of the queen bee herself.

"Anna! Over here!" Maud waved to her from their usual table. "I thought you were going to stand me up."

"Sorry, I'm late, but I promise it's worth it," Anna gushed. "Oh, Riona? I'll have my peppermint tea, please."

Riona could barely keep herself from rolling her eyes at Anna's request. She knew Riona had always looked down on her, down on the entire village, really. She didn't Anna noticed, but she did. It was fine, though; Anna didn't think much of her, either.

"Oh?" Maud's ears pricked up at the prospect of new gossip. "Do tell!"

Anna glanced over her shoulder, wanting to be sure that Riona was going to be there to hear this.

"One peppermint tea," Riona said, placing a tea service for one in front of her. Anna barely acknowledged her.

"I was on my way here from the church, ye know, checking to see if we'd had any more donations for the book and bake sale."

Maud nodded. The book and bake sale was Anna's pride and joy – except for her grandson, Brendan, of course – one she'd started to give people a chance to share in her love of reading, while also making a little money for charity. This year, she'd chosen to donate the funds to fixing the church roof.

"And as I was passing the Flanagans' place, I saw them talking to a mysterious young woman."

Riona acted like she wasn't listening as she cleared a table next to them, but Anna could see how she'd paused for just a second as she picked up a teacup and she knew she was taking in every word.

"She was driving some fancy car and all, too."

"Can I get you more tea, Anna?" Riona interrupted.

"No, thank you, Riona." Anna noticed how the other woman paused a moment too long, like she was debating whether or not to say something.

"Did I hear you say you encountered a stranger over the Flanagans' way?" Riona asked, her tone ringing with a false nonchalance.

Anna preened at having Riona's full attention. Now that she had it, she planned on milking this for as long as she could.

"Yes, she saw a mystery woman up at Dermot and Sinead's place just now on her way here," Maud interrupted.

"A mystery woman? And what did this mystery woman look like?"

"And what's it to you?" Anna asked, raising an eyebrow.

"The Flanagans are my neighbours," Riona replied, as if stating the obvious. "If there's strangers hanging around our part of town, then I feel I should know about it. Can't be too careful these days. Never know who you can trust."

Maud nodded and murmured an agreement while Anna rolled her eyes.

"I don't think you need to worry too much. She was young, mid-twenties, auburn hair. She was driving one of those nice cars, a Lamborghini or Ferrari or something," Anna revealed. She noticed a hint of surprise in Riona's eyes at the mention of the nice car.

"Not the sort of car you'd find around here."

"Indeed."

"And you're sure it wasn't just some relative of Dermot and Sinead's from out of town?"

"I'm sure. The woman called them Mr. and Mrs. Flanagan as she was leaving, and Sinead told her to call them by their names. It's not the sort of thing you'd have to say to someone you're related to."

Riona paused a moment, thinking this over. Anna could see her mind working through the information, then a strange indifference came over her expression. "Probably just some tourist looking for directions or something. I think you've been watching too many of those criminal investigative series, Anna. It's got your imagination all riled up."

She walked back to the counter like she was no longer interested in the conversation, but Anna knew her too well. Riona was planning her own investigation, and she didn't mean to include Anna and Maud in anything she may find.

"Well, that's surprising," Maud commented. "I thought she'd have been much more interested in this news."

"Oh, I think she's very much interested in who this mysterious stranger is. I don't think Riona's given up on solving this one," Anna replied. "Which means you and I need to get a move on and figure this out before she does. Come on, we need to do some investigating."

Anna rose from the table and pulled Maud along with her.

"Where are we going?"

"To where all the good gossip is, of course!"

ഇറ

It was two o'clock on a Tuesday afternoon and, like every other woman in Ballyclara over the age of fifty, Riona Byrne was in O'Sullivan's doing her grocery shopping. For it was a well-known fact that the older generation of Ballyclara women did their shopping on Tuesdays because O'Sullivan's Grocery on a Tuesday afternoon was *the* place to be to get the latest gossip. While the store only had six aisles, it still took each woman over an hour to get their shopping done. This was due in no small part to the fact that, as every woman was inspecting each item before it went into their cart, they conveniently had ample time to listen in to every conversation happening in the next aisle over, and there was no one better at listening in to other people's conversations than Riona Byrne.

As Riona approached the first aisle, she overheard none other than Maud and Anna talking to Nuala O'Shaughnessy.

"Good day, Maud. Anna."

"Good day, Nuala," Maud replied, pleasantly. Riona picked up a small sack of flour, pretending to study its

135

contents label.

"What brings you out today?" Anna asked.

"Oh, ye know, just doing the shopping. And you, as well, I see?"

"Of course."

"Say, I overheard something from Joan Connelly that you met some mystery woman earlier, over by the Flanagans' place. Ye know, I think my Deirdre saw your woman earlier in the pub."

At this, Riona leaned in a little closer.

"Really?" Anna asked. Riona could hear the intrigue in her tone and knew that her mind was likely spinning with all kinds of possibilities. Anna had always fancied herself an amateur sleuth. "What did she say about it?"

There was a pause, as if Nuala was trying to think of exactly what her daughter had told her. "She was at a table with her friends when she came in. Said she looked like she wasn't from around here: nice clothes, nice shoes, and the like. Looked like one of them jackeens, she told me."

A Dubliner. Riona mulled over this information, wondering what this could mean. What was someone from Dublin doing down this way? Was she simply a tourist who'd gotten lost on her way back from Glendalough? Or was she a family member coming to visit?

"A Dubliner, ye say?"

Nuala mumbled something Riona couldn't hear.

"Did she happen to notice if she spoke to anyone or mentioned anything about why she was here?"

"She said she couldn't hear what was said because her table was too far away, and bless her, my daughter's good for many things, but getting gossip from others is not something she's particularly good at. But she did say that she spoke to your Brendan, and Michael Flanagan, as well."

"My Brendan, ye say?"

"Mmhmm."

"Brendan was the one taking her order, but apparently, she requested to talk to Michael. I would have thought your Brendan would've told you about it." There was more than a hint of self-satisfaction in Nuala O'Shaughnessy's voice at having one piece of information that Anna had not, especially since it had concerned Anna's own grandson.

Riona couldn't help but feel a bit of schadenfreude at Anna's expense, too. Riona had always thought her to be a bit too uppity for her liking. She'd tried to get closer to the other women's conversation and moved her cart down the aisle, but in doing so, she failed to notice the small display of cereal boxes at the end of the aisle, and her cart caught the edge, noisily sending the boxes across the floor. Riona immediately felt her cheeks burn with embarrassment. To make matters worse, she heard the click of heels as the other women turned down the aisle to see what the commotion had been.

"Riona? So lovely to see ye. Getting some cereal, are we?" Anna's tone dripped with smugness, knowing that she'd been listening in on their conversation.

"Yes," Riona replied, hurriedly picking up the boxes and putting them back on the display stand. "I mean, no. I was getting some things for the book and bake sale when I bumped into this foolish display. You should mind where you put these things! There's elderly folk who walk down these aisles!" Riona called out loud enough for Mr. O'Sullivan to hear her from his perch behind the cash register.

"Oh, Riona, dear. You shouldn't call yourself elderly," Anna teased.

"I wasn't...I didn't mean me!" Riona replied, insulted.

"Here, let us help you with that." Anna knelt down to pick up some of the boxes and examined them.

"That's not necessary. I can do it." Riona snatched a box out of Anna's hand, wishing she'd just move along.

"It's no problem," Anna replied, looking slightly taken aback at the insistence in Riona's voice. "Oh, I never would have taken you or Aidan for the boxed cereal type." Anna nodded at the box in Riona's hand.

"Oh! No, this is for Karen."

"Oh, really? I had no idea that she was back at home. I thought she and Jimmy were saving for a place of their own. For when the baby comes."

Riona's posture stiffened at the mention of her daughter's boyfriend and her child. She might enjoy nosing around the affairs of others, but she wasn't best pleased about her own family's dirty laundry being aired in public.

"Yes, well, I'm sure she will be soon, and I want to be prepared," she snapped back.

"Of course. Such a shame when a family has a falling out like that." Riona's eyes narrowed at Anna's sickly sweet tone.

"Well, we must be moving on. We need to head over to the pub soon to get things ready for the book and bake sale tomorrow. Oh, and Riona? I hope you had a good listen in to Nuala O'Shaughnessy's information about the mystery woman; it was good stuff. But then, I think you know that."

She gestured to the cereal boxes still on the floor as she pushed the cart along, ushering Maud to follow her to the check-out line, a smug look on her face.

ജ൭

As Mara walked into the pub, she was suddenly yanked aside by her best friend, Molly McCaffrey.

"Don't! Don't go in there," Molly whispered, pulling her towards the far corner by the bar.

"Why not? What's going on?" Mara looked around the busy room, full of people setting up for the book and bake sale Molly's grandmother-in-law organized each year.

"Anna's been trying to corner me all day about some woman who came into the pub the other day. Apparently, Brendan spoke to her when she came in here, and now she thinks I know something about it, even though I was in the kitchen the whole time. Apparently, Michael spoke to her too, so I'd watch out if I were you. She'll be on the hunt for you as well."

"She's been watching those crime shows again, hasn't she?"

"Oh, probably. Ye know what she's like when she thinks she's got a mystery on her hands."

Before Molly could say any more, Anna caught sight of them. "Molly! Mara! There you two are!"

"Oh, no! She's caught sight of us!" Mara looked around her for a possible exit. Brendan's grandmother might look like a sweet old lady, but when she had you cornered, she was a ruthless interrogator.

"Mara, dear, and how's yourself?"

"Um…I'm good, Anna, and you?" she replied, noticing Molly slipping away from the conversation. She tried to motion to her, but Riona Byrne waylaid her on her way to the kitchen. Mara wasn't sure which was worse: dealing with Anna or dealing with Riona.

"Lovely of you to ask, dear. Look, I'm glad I've got ye here for a moment. I wanted to talk to ye about a visitor I saw over at your parents' place. You wouldn't happen to know who it was, would ye?"

"Sorry, no, I don't," Mara replied, truthfully. "She didn't mention it to me when I was over there earlier. Look, I should really get back to helping Molly…"

She noticed Molly had freed herself from Riona and had escaped to the safety of her kitchen.

"Oh, she'll be fine," Anna replied, waving her hand dismissively. "There's loads of people here to give her a hand. Anyways, let's get back to the topic at hand. So, this young woman…"

"I'm really not sure what I can tell ye, Anna. I didn't see her."

"Oh, well, she was a young woman, a little younger than yourself, with auburn hair and she was driving one of them nice sports cars," Anna pressed. "Does that sound like someone ye know? A friend of yours, maybe?"

"No, sorry, Anna. I don't know anyone who fits that description."

"And it's not someone your parents would know?"

"No, I'm pretty sure they don't know anyone that sounds like that, either." Mara smiled apologetically. "Look, I should really help with the set up for your big event…"

"Oh, don't worry about that. So, what about Michael?"

"What about him?" Mara asked, trying to keep the exasperation out of her voice. She was really getting a bit peeved by all these questions, to which she had no answers.

"Well, Nuala O'Shaughnessy's girl, Deirdre, said she saw this young woman ask to talk to Michael. He didn't mention it?"

"No, I'm afraid not. Wish I could be of more help. Here, Moll, let me help you with those."

Molly, who'd reluctantly emerged from the kitchen and was now balancing a couple of boxes of books that had just been brought in. Mara reached out and grabbed a box off the top before it slipped to the floor.

"I can manage," Molly tried to protest, even though she was clearly struggling.

"Believe me, I need the excuse to get away from your grandmother-in-law."

Molly gave her an apologetic look. "Sorry for leaving you with her earlier. If it's any consolation, Riona Byrne cornered me seconds later."

"Yeah, I saw that," Mara replied, placing the books on the table they'd set up. "What did she want?"

"The same thing as Anna, apparently. I think the two of them have some sort of bet going on as to who's going to find out the identity of this mystery woman first, or at least why she was here."

"She was probably just some tourist," Mara shrugged, setting up some books for display.

"Could've been," Molly agreed. "But it's kind of weird that she would've gone out to your parents' place. I mean, yours and Michael's cottages are first on that road. If she'd gotten lost, wouldn't she have stopped in at one of your places first?"

"Well, Anna said that she was talking to Michael here, so she wouldn't have stopped in at his place. And I was probably out at a job, so maybe she just kept going until she saw my parents' car in the drive and stopped in there. I mean, the only other house on that road is the Old Rectory and no one's lived there for years."

Molly glanced at her out of the corner of her eye.

"And which happens to be for sale."

Mara puzzled over the comment for a second before realizing where she was going with her train of thought. "You don't think she's planning to buy the place, do you?"

"Well, it makes sense. Your parents are the ones who are in charge of the sale, and by the sounds of this woman, she'd have the kind of money needed to buy the place and fix it up."

"Well now, that's an interesting thought. I think you and I have just stumbled upon the answer to this big mystery everyone's so stuck on." She winked at Molly conspiratorially.

"Well, *I* solved the mystery," Molly pointed out. "You just happened to be here when it happened."

Mara playfully punched her in the arm.

"What are you two so happy about?" Maud asked, sneaking up behind them, carrying a small box of books.

"Mrs. Drummond! We didn't see you there." Mara felt her heart leap at having been surprised by the older woman.

"Oh, we were just playing around," Molly replied quickly. "Here, let us take that. We'll put those on display for you."

Maud smiled as she relinquished her box and headed back over to where Anna was directing Nuala and Deirdre O'Shaughnessy, who were helping to put up some of the decorations for the event.

"You don't think she heard us, do you?" Mara asked, observing the older women as they chatted.

"It's hard to tell. If she did, Maud wouldn't be one to hide it from Anna. Those two are inseparable. But, if she did just tell her what she overheard, I'd think Anna would seem more...excited. I'd think she wouldn't be able to resist immediately marching over to Riona to rub it in her face."

"In any case, I should probably go up to Mam's place and warn her, just to be sure. Do you mind if I cut out a little early?"

"No, go on! I've got you covered. Besides, don't you have that landscaping meeting in an hour?"

"Right! Thanks for the reminder. What would I do without you?"

"You'd be hopelessly lost," Molly teased her.

Mara smiled at her as she headed out of the pub towards her parents' place. Twenty minutes later, she was standing on their doorstep.

"Oh, hello, dear!" Sinead greeted her daughter. "Was I expecting you?"

"I wanted to come over to remind you about Rory coming over to yours tonight for his tea because I've got that meeting about the landscaping job over on the Ballinacor Estate at three."

"Oh, that's right! Of course, he can. Any excuse to spend time with our grandson." Sinead smiled at her, setting up some baking ingredients in front of her and tying an apron around her waist.

"Doing some baking for the book sale tomorrow?" Mara asked.

"Yes, I thought I'd bake some pies to sell. Speaking of which, weren't you supposed to be down at the pub today helping to set up?"

"Yeah, I just came from there." Mara paused a moment, watching her mother mixing the ingredients. "You're the talk of the whole village, ye know."

"Is that so?" Her mother seemed completely oblivious to this, but Mara could see through the pretense.

"Don't play coy with me, Mam. What's all this

about some mystery woman coming over the other day?
And why is everyone so interested in her?"

"I'm sure, and I wouldn't know why everyone is so
interested in this mystery woman you're talking about."

"So, there *was* some stranger here the other day."

"I didn't say that," Sinead replied calmly, little puffs
of flour rising from the countertop where she was kneading dough.

"Yes, you just did. I asked you two questions:
what's all this about the mystery woman, and why is everyone so interested in her? You only answered the second
one because it's the only one you could answer without
lying to me."

Sinead sighed and stopped kneading her dough for
a moment. "What time did ye say you had that meeting
at?"

"Three o'clock. Don't change the subject."

"Well, you'd better get a move on if you want to
make it on time. It's already half-two." Sinead nodded towards the clock on the wall.

Mara double-checked on her mobile. "Shoot! I've
got to run, but don't think this gets you off the hook. I'm
not done with you yet. I see you, and I know there's
plenty you're not telling me."

Mara headed out the back door, then paused and
turned around to look at her mother one last time.

"Oh, go on with ye!" Sinead sighed, with more than
a hint of exasperation. "You're starting to sound too
much like Anna McCaffrey! You think everything's one
big mystery!"

Mara smirked at her and pulled out her mobile on
her way to her car, calling Molly.

"Molly? Yeah, it's Mara. I talked to Mam, and she
definitely knows something. I didn't get much out of her;

only confirmed that there *was* a stranger over at the house the other day, but we're definitely on the right track."

ℰℭ

Maud Drummond had most certainly overheard what Mara and Molly had been talking about at the pub earlier and, like Molly had said, had gone straight to Anna about it. Which is how Anna now found herself on Sinead Flanagan's doorstep. Seeing Sinead through the kitchen window, she knocked swiftly on the back door and waited.

"Well, hello there, Anna. This is a surprise. Come in, come in."

While she was certainly pleasant enough, there was something in her countenance that made Anna certain that she wasn't entirely pleased to see her, but was being too polite to say so.

"What brings you this way?"

"I was just down at the pub setting up for the book and bake sale tomorrow when I noticed Mara had left her jacket. Molly said that she'd left a bit early for some meeting, so I thought I'd come up here and try to return it to her before she left."

"I'm afraid you just missed her," Sinead replied, brushing her floured hands on her apron. "She had a meeting over on the Ballinacor Estate, but thank ye for returning it. I'll be sure she gets it."

Sinead reached out for the jacket, but Anna held onto it a moment longer, wanting to seize the opportunity to press Sinead further on the case of the auburn-haired stranger, but was waylaid by the smell of smoke wafting through the air and the piercing sound of the smoke alarm.

"The pies!" Sinead exclaimed. "Thank ye for coming over, Anna. I'll see you tomorrow."

Sinead took Mara's jacket from her hands and firmly directed Anna to the back step, shutting the door behind her with a heavy thud.

"Well, now," Anna said to the misty, cool air. She may have been deterred from interrogating her prime suspect, but Anna considered herself a patient woman. She'd find another time to corner Sinead and get the truth out of her.

ഔൣ

It was the day of the book and bake sale and, as the organizer, Anna couldn't be prouder of how it had turned out.

"Excellent work, Anna."

"Great turnout!" Deirdre O'Shaughnessy told her as she passed by.

Anna practically glowed from all the praise. There was just one thing that was still nagging at her.

"So, Sinead, about this woman who was at yours the other day..." she started, noticing Sinead standing on her own for the first time that day. Anna was determined to get her answers one way or the other and determine the case closed on this mystery.

Sinead sighed and exclaimed, "Alright! Enough about it already!"

Then, breaking away from Anna and the rest of the crowd, she climbed up onto the little stage near the front of the pub. She tapped the mic, sending a loud screeching sound of feedback throughout the building, commanding everyone's attention.

"I want everyone to listen in real closely now so that you all get the information at the same time. Yes, there's been an offer made on the Old Rectory, and yes, it's a young woman from Dublin. And no, I don't have any further details for ye because the sale isn't final just yet, so you can all just stop making such a big fuss over it all."

The room fell silent for a millisecond, then exploded with a cacophony of questions.

"What's the woman's name?"

"Will she be tearing the old place down?"

"Will she be moving here permanently?"

"She's not one of them jackeens who's only going to be using the place as a weekend home, is she?"

"Ugh, those are the worst."

"When will she be moving in?"

"She's going to be a load of trouble; just you mark my words."

Sinead stepped down off the stage, an exasperated expression on her face. "Are ye happy now, Anna?"

And Anna *was* happy now. Happy that she'd been the one who brought to light the Mystery of the Auburn-Haired Woman, and it was she who'd solved it. And now, it was case closed on the Mystery of the Auburn-Haired Woman.

Did you like *Tales from Ballyclara*? Leave a review!

Tales from Ballyclara can be found on the review site of your choice.

Read more from Erin Bowlen:

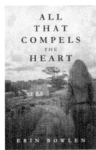  

The Aoife O'Reilly series is a collection of bestselling women's fiction novels from Canadian author, Erin Bowlen. With its deeply drawn characters and slow-burn chemistry, you'll love this moving journey. Click the images above to begin reading now!

About the Author

Erin Bowlen is the author of the best-selling Aoife O'Reilly series.

Erin was born and raised in New Brunswick, Canada. Growing up, she was influenced by her family's artistic roots in both music and storytelling. She began her writing career during her postgraduate studies in Classics at the University of New Brunswick.

In 2018, she published her first novel in the best-selling Aoife O'Reilly series, *All That Compels the Heart*.

In 2020, she published the second novel in the series, *Where I'm Home*, as well as the #1 best-selling prequel novella, *Grainne*.

Erin currently lives in New Brunswick.

.